A TIME AND A PLACE

Alfred A Knopf
New York   *1 9 6 8*

A TIME
AND
A PLACE

Stories by

William Humphrey

THIS IS A BORZOI BOOK
PUBLISHED BY ALFRED A. KNOPF, INC.

First Edition

Copyright © 1963, 1965, 1967, 1968
by William Humphrey

"The Ballad of Jesse Neighbours" first appeared in
ESQUIRE MAGAZINE *in September 1963.*
"A Voice from the Woods" first appeared in the
ATLANTIC MONTHLY *in October 1963.*
"The Pump" first appeared in
ESQUIRE MAGAZINE *in December 1963.*
"A Good Indian" first appeared under a different title in
THE SATURDAY EVENING POST *in August 1965.*
"A Job of the Plains" first appeared in the Twentieth Anni-
versary Issue of the QUARTERLY REVIEW OF LITERATURE *in 1965.*
"The Rainmaker" first appeared in
THE SATURDAY EVENING POST *in December 1967.*
"A Home Away from Home" first appeared in
THE SATURDAY EVENING POST *in September 1968.*
"The Human Fly" first appeared in
ESQUIRE MAGAZINE *in September 1968.*
"The Last of the Caddoes" first appeared in
ESQUIRE MAGAZINE *in October 1968.*
"Mouth of Brass" appears for the first time in this collection.

Library of Congress Catalog Card Number: 68–31608
Manufactured in the United States of America

To my friend Theodore Weiss

CONTENTS

A TIME AND A PLACE

The Ballad of Jesse Neighbours

FEW MARRIAGES were being made in Oklahoma in 1934 and Jesse Neighbours didn't have a pot nor a window to throw it out of, but Jesse just couldn't wait. Things might never get any better! He had to have her—Naomi Childress, that is. What were they going to live on, love? Well, they would have each other and they would scrape by somehow. Things couldn't go on like this much longer. Meanwhile, two can live cheaper than one. And Naomi didn't expect any diamond rings.

Jesse was just twenty, though he looked older, and Naomi just eighteen. In the road of their courtship there had been one bad bump. It was the old story: poor boy, heiress, and her father. Jesse's people had never owned one red acre to sit back now and watch being blown away in dust. Will Neighbours had raised, rather was raising, seven children, Jesse the eldest, as a sharecropper. And so from the first Jesse had had to come to the Childresses hat in hand. For old Bull Childress had a house and clear title to

3

twenty-seven acres of hardscrabble. The deed was unencumbered through no fault of Bull's. He had tried, but nobody would loan him anything on that patch of Jimson weeds and cockleburs.

Bull's consent to the marriage had been given only on condition that the bride be taken to a home of her own, and not to live with her in-laws. And indeed to have gotten another into Will's place they would have had to hang her on a nail at night. Bull's provision might have proved an insuperable obstacle. But fortunately Jesse was the son of a man known for hard work and honesty; and though only twenty, Jesse himself, after some ten years now, was beginning to earn a name as a steady worker. And so Mr. Buttrell, Will's landlord, agreed to try Jesse on shares on a place that he happened to have standing vacant.

Not a very big place, and maybe not the best thirty acres left in Oklahoma, but a place of his own and land which a strong young fellow not afraid of a little work could make out on—always barring Acts of God, of course —with a two-room dog-run cabin, a well, a barn, a toolshed, and a chicken house. Jesse had a heifer due to freshen around September and Naomi was raising a dozen layers that she had incubated underneath the kitchen range. There would be a pair of shoats as a wedding present from Will. The two of them were spending every spare moment fixing the place up. It would have curtains made from the pretty flowered prints that chicken feed came sacked in, and all that winter a quilt on a quilting frame had hung above the dining table in the Childresses' parlor, and the neighbor women came over every Thursday afternoon and quilted on it, and made jokes about it that made Naomi's round and sweetly fuzzy cheeks glow like a ripe Elberta peach. And she was canning all that previous summer and fall as if she had three hands. If nothing else they would be able to live on cucumber pickles. Jesse had

4

an old car. Something was always going wrong with it, but luckily Jesse had a second one exactly like the first, except for the lack of wheels, which squatted out in the front yard, a sort of personal parts dep't, very handy. He had given up smoking and instead was putting his tobacco money in a jar, and by fall he hoped to have enough to make a down payment on a mule. He was the saving kind, saved tinfoil, twine, saved rubber bands, making large balls of all three items which he stored in cigar boxes.

Naomi knew what a catch she had made. She had first taken serious notice of Jesse Neighbours one night at a country dance for which he supplied the music. He hired out around the section as a one-man band. He had a rig which he was buying on installment from the mail-order catalogue. Once in it he looked like a monkey in a cage. With his hands he played guitar while with his feet he worked two pedals on which were drumsticks that banged a pair of snare drums; one stick was bare wood, the other was covered like a swab with bright-orange lamb's wool. A French harp was held to his mouth on a wire frame with earpieces. The boy was a musical fool. In his pockets he always carried some kind of musical instrument: a jew's harp, a French harp, an ocarina. He played the musical saw, the washboard, water glasses, blew a jug. He could draw music out of anything. And on the guitar or the banjo or the mandolin he picked notes, not just chords but whole tunes. His singing voice was like a bee in a bottle, a melodious, slightly adenoidal whine, wavering, full of sobs and breaks, and of a pitch like a boy's before the change of voice. That night when he laid aside the French harp and sang:

> "I don't want your greenback dollar;
> I don't want your watch and chain;
> All I want is you, my darling;
> Won't you take me back again?"

5

it seemed to Naomi that he was singing to her alone. And when with his next number he showed the other, light side of his nature with *Sal, Sal, Sal, oh, Sal, Sal, let me chaw yore rozin some,* then Naomi was hooked. And Naomi was not the only one, as she very well knew.

But the music he courted her with was none of his lovesick ballads. Seated on her front porch on a Sunday afternoon, in his fresh-ironed khakis so stiff they squeaked, his chauffeur's black leather bow tie fluttering on his Adam's apple as he sang like a black butterfly, he would throw back his head and bawl:

> "I heard the crash on the highway.
> I knew what it was from the start.
> I rushed to the scene of destruction.
> The picture was stamped on my heart.

> I didn't hear nobody pray, dear brethren,
> I didn't hear nobody pray.
> The blood lay thick on the highway,
> But I didn't hear nobody pray."

For it was bad enough already, him being landless. If on top of that he had come around strumming and crooning ballads and ditties old Bull Childress would have shooed him out of the yard like a stray dog. Bull would think, any fellow that played all that well, not just chords but notes, must have spent a lot of time sitting in the shade learning to pick them out, and that was not the kind a man wanted for a son-in-law. The truth was, Jesse had spent very little time learning; it just came naturally. But of course he could not say that. The pious wail of *The Crash on the Highway* was meant to overcome a prospective father-in-law's misgivings.

And Jesse was not shiftless. He was a most unusual combination of music and prudence. His music meant a little extra money. He liked to play and sing, and in fact

6

his foot was always tapping to some tune running in his head; but he liked to be paid for it too. He was ambitious. He meant to get ahead. He was already thinking of a family of his own, thinking of it with a passion beyond his years, and notwithstanding her blushes, he broached the subject very early to Naomi. He spoke of it with such earnestness that she had to say at last, she hoped he was not thinking of quite as big a one as his own. It had not occurred to her that, however many there were, he meant to bring them up in a very different way from the way he and his brothers and sisters had been brought up.

Though it might be hard to understand why a young fellow should want to follow in his father's footsteps when his father's only followed in those of a mule, and why he should want to do it in order to own something which the wind blew away in clouds of red dust before your very eyes, Jesse Neighbours meant to own land of his own one day. Not that he couldn't wait. Not that his longing made him discontent with what he was starting out with. But stumbling along behind the plow among the blocks of dirt like chunks of concrete paving, straining against the handles, grunting, his face caked with dust, he would let himself think of the future. He was of an age and a seriousness to have a place in the councils of family men, farmers, and on the corner of the street in town on Saturday afternoon Jesse had heard it said time and time again that this land was cottoned out. Well, he meant to rotate his crops. He would have a margin of land over what he needed in order to just get by, enough to quarter his acreage and leave one quarter to lie fallow by turns each year. Then there was the weather. A man might have a good year, but then one of drought could wipe out all that he had saved. The weather, they said, was one thing you could do nothing about. But there was one thing you could do. You could grow one crop that did not depend so heavily

7

on the weather. Jesse had heard those same men say that this land, once the range of the buffalo, was best suited to grazing. He meant to have a little herd of beef cattle one day. He knew already what breed. Bramers. Funny-looking things, they were, with that white hide like a scalded hog, that hump on the back like a camel, and those great flopping ears. And mean! But they were from India and could stand this Oklahoma heat and dryness like no others, and fever ticks never bothered them. Jesse didn't fool himself: he would never own any big herd. That was for men with capital, not for the likes of him. He would always be a dirt farmer. But a few he would have; then in a year when there came a drought or a hailstorm, or worst of all, when the crop was so good the bottom fell out of the market price, then you wouldn't have to go crawling to the bank and lick spit and put yourself in hock right up to your very eyeballs.

And though he would be a clodhopper all his days, if he started a little herd his sons wouldn't have to slave like this, daylight to dark, seven days a week, just to keep body and soul together; they could be cattlemen, breeders. Patience, he would need patience to save and then save more, until he could buy good stock, blooded, purebred, pedigreed —it paid off in the long run. And, sweat pouring from his face like rainwater off a hatbrim as he hunched himself, he drove the plowshare back into the stony ground and swore at the wheezing mule, thinking as he lurched down the row, if a man started out with one heifer, bred her and was lucky and she had twins and they were both heifers, and each of them had a heifer . . . So that he never heard his little sister until she was at his back, though all the way down from the house she had been screaming at the top of her lungs that they'd struck oil on the Childress place.

Oil-well derricks on those Oklahoma plains were a commoner sight than trees. New ones sprang up, old ones

8

were drilled deeper, with every fresh discovery of oil any-
where within a hundred miles. Bad times and bad soil bred
them like weeds, where no edible plant would grow. The
lucky ones struck water, and the derrick was converted
into a windmill. Even Bull Childress had long since given
up hope of anything from that one down behind his house.
Jesse had forgotten it so completely that for a moment he
hardly knew what his little sister was talking about.

"They claim it's a real gusher, Jess," she said. "The
Childresses are rich! Naomi's going to be one of them mil-
lionairesses, like you read about in the newspapers."

Even as she spoke her voice ran down like a phonograph, seeing the look in her brother's eyes, blank holes in
the terra-cotta mask of his face. Her mouth gaped, snaggle-
toothed, as it dawned on her that the news she had brought
might not be good news, after all.

Jesse leaned for a moment on the plow handles, breathing hard, his head sagging between his shoulder blades,
sweat dripping from the tip of his nose. He spat thinly and
of the color of blood and wiped the back of his gritty hand
across his lips. Then he straightened, and settling the reins
about his neck, grasping the handles and pointing the plowshare downward again, he said in a dry husky voice, "Come
up, mule."

The story told was that the well blew in while old Bull
was in the outhouse looking at the pictures in the unused
pages of the mail-order catalogue, and that when she let
go he shot off the hole and out the door with his flap hanging open and his britches down around his knees, tripped
and sprawled flat on his face, rolled over, looked up, and
then lay there moaning with joy and letting the slimy,
thick, foul-smelling black rain spatter in his face and into
his open mouth like sweet California wine. The roar was

a steady explosion and the stink enough to make you gag. Air to breathe there was none and the sky turned black as in a dust storm. And as he lay there Bull's moaning turned insensibly into a whimper, a sob, as he thought of the years of his life that had gone into that hard, unyielding soil, the sweat from his hanging brow that had watered every inch of it, of the furrows he had broken, the cotton sacks he had dragged across it, bent double beneath the broiling sun, the seed he had sown in it and which had rotted there, never sprouting. Of this dry red dirt he had eaten his allotted peck, and more. His head was bent to it like an ear on an undernourished stalk; his skin had taken on its very color like a stain. And all this while deep underground lay this black treasure. And rolling over he commenced to beat the earth with his fists for having hidden its riches from him all his life until now. Then when he had exhausted himself beating it, he flung his arms wide in an embrace and kissed the ground again and again.

In the house he found his daughter trying to pull down the windows and his wife cursing over her wash that had been hanging on the line and that now looked like a heap of mechanic's rags. Aghast at her blasphemous complaints, Bull roared, "You'll wear silks and laces from now on, you old fool! Shut your mouth and thank the good Lord! Don't let Him hear you grumbling!" And grabbing up the laundry he flung it to the floor and danced on it with his bare black feet, bellowing jubilantly.

All afternoon it rained down and Bull hopped from one window to the next, crowing, "Spew, baby, spew! Oh, honey, don't never stop! Flood us! Drown us in it! Oh, Godawmighty, blow her sky high! Let it come down for forty days and forty nights!" Three times in the course of the afternoon he dashed outdoors like a boy in a summer shower and baptized himself anew, letting it dance in his open palms and blacken his upturned face, and in that

10

state he would return, tracking up the floors, and demand a hug and kiss from each of his women, chasing them screaming through the house.

All night long it fell like a spring rain on the noisy sheet-iron roof, and the stench grew hellish. But Bull lay unsleeping in his bed, smacking his old woman's flat bony behind whenever he suspected her of dozing off, listening to the patter overhead and crooning, "Oh, keep it up, sweet Jesus. Oh, pour it down. Don't never stop till I tell you."

Towards daybreak the next morning the crew succeeded in capping the well, and they ventured out to have a look around. The world looked burnt, smelled burnt too. From the eaves of buildings, from the handles of tools long abandoned about the yard, from the limp leaves of trees and plants the black syrup hung in long slow-swelling drops. From the sagging fence wires they were strung in ropes like beads and amid the leaves of bushes they resembled small poisonous black berries. From every blade of grass, like a viscous black dew, hung a single unfalling drop. A dying songbird staggered about the yard, his wings heavy and useless. Upon the pool in the bottom of the cast-iron washpot lay insects in a thick, still crust.

"Won't nothing ever grow here ever again," Mrs. Childress wailed, seeing her dead peonies and the earth around them that looked as if it had been tarred and asphalted.

"I hope to God not!" cried Bull. "I done raised all the crops I ever aim to off of it!"

Breakfast (oily biscuits, coffee that tasted like it had been drained from a crankcase) was hardly over when Bull said, "Well, gals, yawl take off your aprons and paint your faces. The Childresses are headed for the big city. Don't bother packing nothing. We won't need none of this trash" —the sweep of his arm comprehended the sum of their previous life—"never no more."

So they piled into the cab of the truck (a pickup, cut

down from a La Salle sedan) and took off. In town they stopped just long enough for Bull to go to the bank, from which he returned carrying two bulging canvas sacks, and after that they never even slowed down for Idabel, nor even Paris, but drove straight to Dallas, with old Bull sitting on that horn all the way. And when they got there they drove straight to the Adolphus, pulled up out front, and though they had not brought one piece of luggage with them, sat there honking until the whole corps of bellhops and porters had been sent out to receive them. When they got out, so did the broody hen who had made the trip with them unbeknownst. She staggered off her nest among the corn shucks and croaker sacks in the truck bed, and out into the street, and there she died, in a shower of feathers and with a bloodcurdling squawk, underneath the wheels of a new red Ford V-8, right on the corner of Commerce and Akard.

Without turning his head, jerking his thumb over his shoulder at the old jitney, Bull said to the head greeter, "Get shut of that for me, will you? Maybe you know some poor devil that can use it."

They were not turned away. They were welcomed like royalty. After Corsicana, after Spindletop, after Kilgore, Dallas had developed a keen collective nose for crude oil, and rolled out the red carpet for their kind of barefoot millionaire. Bull drew his X on the register as big as a level-crossing sign.

And at Neiman-Marcus that same afternoon they seemed to have been expecting Naomi. To her request for a permanent wave and "a beauty treatment," they smiled, and showed her in. She was undressed and popped into a box with her head sticking out like a turkey's at a turkey shoot, parboiled, removed feeling as if she had been peeled and her quick exposed, stretched out on a white table and kneaded like dough until her bones jellied and her brains melted and ran. She was put into a white gown and whisked into a second chamber, seated in a dentist's chair, and mud, or what certainly seemed like mud, piled on her face. To soft music wafted sourcelessly in, a bevy of sibilant attendants busied themselves about her, one to each foot, one to each hand, plying, chafing, clipping. The mud was removed, then came lotions icy and astringent, a brisk facial massage, a shampoo. The head beautician materialized, a gorgeous young sorcerer of intermediate sex with bangs and plucked brows, a pout, fluttering hands smaller and whiter and far softer than Naomi's own, a voice like molasses in January and a pettish toss of the head. From a palette of rosy tints he chose, and with brushes and swabs applied them to Naomi's cheeks, frowning, standing back from time to time to squint at her like an artist before his easel. Her head was anointed with the contents of various vials, her hair cut and curled.

At last it was finished and she was permitted to look. One glimpse and she looked about for confirmation. They nodded. She looked again, sidelong, scared. She reached out a hand (once, or rather always, red and cracked from lye soap, cold water, broom handles, the bails of buckets —now white, soft, a row of small pointed flames burning at the finger tips) and shyly touched the vision in the glass. Her lips parted in wonder, her lips that had blossomed, sweetly sullen, moist, quivering. Wonder, not self-infatuation, was what she felt, for that was not her, it was a creature from another world, out of the pages of *Silver Screen*, beautiful as a dummy in a store window. Her hair was a platinum cloud. Her eyes had doubled in size. Beneath lids elongated and shaded with blue, the whites sparkled, the pupils swooned within themselves, liquid with promise and cruel caprice. Her brows had been resettled; they arched of themselves. Sophistication had been shadowed into her hitherto round and girlish cheeks.

To maintain this new beauty of hers, regular and frequent return visits would be necessary. Meanwhile there were certain ointments and extracts of which she herself was to make nightly application, according to a ritual which she would be taught. This cream, from the beestings of wild Mongolian she-asses. This, with ambergris secreted by afflicted whales and found floating upon tropical seas. A hair rinse of champagne and plovers' eggs. This jelly rich in the hormones of queen bees fed on the nectar of Alpine wild flowers. This lotion, to prevent dry skin, containing morning dew from the Sahara. Miracles of modern science and ancient recipes, the guarded secrets of Cleopatra and the Queen of Sheba, precious as virgin's milk, reserved for the world's privileged few fair women.

When she had been metamorphosed Naomi was shown the raiment she was to wear in her new station. In a mirrored room carpeted like spring grass haughty models paraded for her private pleasure. Naked ones—no, not naked, clothed in lingerie so diaphanous as to seem to be. Then dressed in spidery lace, silk as fine as smoke, scratchy tweeds to tickle the skin and suave satins to soothe it. Leathers supple and scaly, of reptiles and birds and unborn calves. Furs from every corner of the globe, Andean chinchilla that shrank shyly from the touch as if still alive, sleek otter, marten, mink and sable, ermine fluffy as thistledown, velvety clipped beaver, smooth leopard, kinky karakul. Around their svelte necks they wore ropes of pearls, chains of icy-green emeralds, around their thin wrists that had never wrung out a mop, bracelets of diamonds and rubies and gold, tiny watches that imprisoned time and kept them eternally young. The bills were to be sent to her daddy, Mr. O. B. Childress, care of the Adolphus Hotel.

"The Hotel Adolphus?" said the lady.

"That's right," said Naomi; and that night she was able to correct her mother's pronunciation: the accent in "hotel" fell on the second syllable.

14

They stayed a week, saw the zoo, the aquarium, went to a nightclub, and took all their meals in restaurants.

The new Packard was delivered to the door at the hour of their departure. It was mustard-colored; the seats, upholstered in red leather, looked like davenports. And though it was as long as a hearse, when the porters had brought down all the hatboxes and shoe boxes and boxed dresses and coats and suits and piled them on the sidewalk and started packing the car, it was evident that they would never get it all in. So Bull telephoned the dealer and another Packard, identical twin to the first, was brought over. As he was the only one in the family who could drive, Bull turned to the manager, who had come out to bid them goodbye, and said, pointing to one of the porters, "What'll you take for that boy there? And throw in his uniform?" The porter couldn't drive either. He could steer, though, and that was how the Childresses returned home, one car hitched behind the other.

Jesse did not expect any word from Naomi, and it was not just that he believed her father would forbid her to send him any. The lore of his class, the songs he sang, were rich in cynical commentaries on such situations as his. He cursed her and dismissed her from his mind. Or told himself he had. But the first time he saw her on the street, and she passed him by as if afraid of dirtying herself by looking at him, though he tried to despise her new clothes they frightened him instead, and her new hairdo and those little refinements of carriage that she was already exhibiting all made her so beautiful that he was smitten as never before. The scent she left behind her in the street broke his heart. And he might as well have been dead for all she cared. Not a word. Not a glance. Not even for old times' sake.

Meanwhile, following Bull Childress's strike, the oil

fever hit the section, and it seemed to poor Jesse that everybody except his folks had a piece of ground big enough to
drill a hole and sink a pipe; only they had none. Land
prices began to skyrocket, and there went the other dream
of Jesse's life. Land that always, until now, had gone beg-
ging at twenty dollars an acre, land that had sold for unpaid taxes and gone unsold even for that, was suddenly
fetching thousands of dollars. He alone owned none. Now
he never would.

Clyde Barrow and Bonnie Parker were dead, the Texas
badman and his gun moll. The town, one Saturday just
past noon when Jesse joined his gang of buddies on Main
Street, pullulated with the news. Dead. Clyde Barrow and
Bonnie Parker. It had happened some days before (the
previous Wednesday, in fact) but it was news, for if like
Jesse and most of the others on the streets you spent Monday through Saturday morning behind a plow talking only
to a mule, it was in town on Saturday afternoon that you
caught up on the week's events. Clyde and Bonnie. Dead.
The groups of men collected on the corners were both subdued and excited, with an air at once conspiratorial and
challenging, as if defying a ban on public gatherings; and
as with the people of an occupied country, when a partisan
hero (and heroine), one of their own, had been caught
and executed by the authorities, the flag of their traditional,
classless, blood sympathy with the outlaw flew at half-
mast.

The folk hero, in yet another avatar, was dead, and already the prose of their lament was growing cadenced and
incantatory, half on its way to being verse, and soon would
be music, and then, in the cotton fields, to the rhythm of
the chopping of a hoe, on records in café nickelodeons, on
street corners sung by blind, legless veterans to the whang

of a steel guitar, young men would be adjured to take warning and listen to me, and told his story. How he was a poor boy—and thus already, even before his first recorded infraction (which had been to defend his sister's honor against a rich lecher, or the theft from hunger of a dime loaf of bread, or through impatience with the law's delay in righting a wrong which he, a poor boy, had suffered) on the outs with the law. A poor boy, alone, against the world, and orphaned. Orphaned of a father, that is; for a mother there would be, old and ailing, to visit whom in her illness he regularly slipped through the cordon of deputies and marshals posted around the family homestead with the loose insolent ease of a nocturnal panther. A poor boy who died young; handsome it went without saying; with women by the score ready to die for him, and one who gained immortality by dying with him. And a man (already in the barber shops and around the marble machines in the cafés they were wondering how the law could have known that Clyde would come down that road at that hour that day, he whose every move had been as stealthy and as sly as a hunted coyote, they who for two years he had made look like monkeys), a bosom friend, the one man he had ever taken into his confidence, whose life perhaps, which is to say undoubtedly, he had saved, ready to kiss his cheek in public for a handful of silver.

The actual place it had happened was in Louisiana, where, as their car passed through a narrow and bushy defile, they had been jumped, ambushed, by a party of local and out-of-state lawmen, who opened fire with shotguns, pistols, and automatic rifles. The car in the picture looked like a colander and the bodies of a thin, undersized young man and a thin young woman, who even in death retained the lean and sinewy wariness of an alley cat, looked like wild game, the lawmen standing over them with their guns, posing with stiff proud smiles, as in those photographs of hunting parties with the day's trophies lying at their feet. "I hated to bust a cap on a woman," the gallant leader of the posse was quoted as saying. "Especially when she was sitting down. But if it wouldn't of been her it would of been us."

And so at last it had come: the end to a reign of terror throughout the whole Southwest of some two years, as the newspapers put it. The end which had been expected daily and its every detail long foreseen (he would go out blazing, would take as many with him as he could, if they gave him a chance, which they didn't, and her too, old cigar-smoking Bonnie too, would never surrender, not Clyde, but would, should it come to that, save one last cartridge, or rather two, for themselves) had been foreseen and almost already lived through, yet never for one moment believed in, and secretly prayed against, even by those holding what they considered the sure number in the betting pools that had been made on the date.

And already, in the barbers' chairs beneath the turbaned mounds of towels, on the shoeshine stands, to the click of snooker balls, in the otherwise unused (except as a kind of local Salvation Army shelter for the town's two incorrigible and hopeless drunks) waiting room of the depot, hanging around waiting for old 88 to howl through and fling off the mail sack, they were saying: a dozen of them, and after two years of being made to look like a pack of fools, against one man and a girl! And without even giving them a chance to surrender (when what they meant was, without giving them a fighting chance to return fire). And saying that when the bodies were taken from the car (he had been at the wheel) she was found to have died in the act of drawing her pistol—not no lady's purse popgun but a real sonofabitching honest-to-by-God old .45 government-issue Colt automatic—from the glove compartment. And maybe her kind was what had led that poor boy astray in the first place, but she had stuck by her man, I God, through thick and thin, you had to say that for Bonnie Parker, she had stuck by her man.

And then—a note of state pride in the voice then, and a dry cackle of a snort—"I God, they ain't caught Purty Boy yit!" Meaning Oklahoma's own Pretty Boy Floyd. And how there was a man—not mentioning no names, but if you was to, why, it wouldn't be the first time they ever heard it, and he lived not so very far away—that answered a knock on the farmhouse door late one cold and rainy winter night and called *Who's there?* and got back for answer *A friend,* and opened the door and held the lamp up to a handsome young face that he had never seen before except on the wall alongside the rental boxes in the post office, but had said *Come in, friend,* for he had been honored by the title, been proud to give him the night's lodging he asked for, and had turned the kids out despite his protests and made them down a pallet on the floor, and next morning had found, or his wife had, pinned to the blanket a one-hundred-dollar bill. And that man was not the only man in Oklahoma that such a tale might tell. Not none of these biggety new oil-rich that up to six months ago had always wiped on a cob and now tried to look as if they never wiped at all, but them that still knew what it was to be a poor boy and on the outs with the law—which two things came to the same.

And someone wondered, for sooner or later someone was bound to, if it really was Clyde and Bonnie in that car. For the law shot first and asked questions later, and never confessed afterwards to any little mistakes of theirs. And they had been made to look mighty foolish for a long time. And they could use the bodies of a young man and a young woman, too shot up to be really identified, for public consumption. And that led to talk of the greatest badman of them all. How a man, an old-timer, had turned up in Oklahoma City, or maybe it was Tulsa, not so very long ago, claiming he was Jesse James and could prove it, and that the dirty little coward who in the song had shot Mr. Howard and laid poor Jesse in his grave, had done no such thing, only it had been convenient at the time to let it be thought so.

And our Jesse listened, smiling bashfully, the black leather bow tie riding up his Adam's apple as he ducked his chin, reddening a little, as one must when a hero is being spoken of who shares one's name.

And they talked of other storied outlaws past and present, of Baby Face Nelson and Dillinger, of Sam Bass and Billy the Kid, and always, here among Jesse's crowd in particular, the word "poreboy," "a poreboy," sounded, like the bass string which the hand must always strum no matter what the chord, on a guitar. A poreboy who had got himself into a little trouble, and was maltreated and made mean by the law because he was a poreboy with nothing and nobody to buy them off, whom they might club and rubber-hose with impunity, a poreboy with no one to go his bail. For the gang that Jesse squatted and whittled and spat with in town on Saturday afternoon was different now from his former companions. Instead of the older, steadier (and as he now thought of them, cowed and beaten) family men, he hung out now with a group of young men of all ages, bachelors married and unmarried, hired hands and tenant farmers' sons from off the land and young mechanics and day laborers from the town and those without any fixed address nor visible means of support traceable origins who spent the days between Saturdays sitting along the loading platform of the cotton compress or in the domino parlor, those left out of the current oil boom, who made vague threats every now and then of running off and joining the Navy. And always in their telling there was a woman in it, too, at the root of it always some woman, one for whose sake a poreboy had gone wrong, and who, if she had not actually sold him out, had deserted him when the chips were down. As in the ballad, merely one of the most popular of hundreds on the theme, which had become Jesse's favorite among his repertoire:

I got no use for the women.
A true one can never be found.
They'll stick by a man while he's winning;
When he's losing they turn him down.

Except for passing showers lasting half an hour, and leaving upon the parched soil a crust like dried blood, it was six weeks since rain had fallen. The sun swooped lower by the day, singeing the stunted cotton like feathers in a flame. There was not even dew by night to settle the dust that choked the air. Men's heads were commencing to shake. It looked as if they were headed into another summer like the last, and the one before that.

In all of Oklahoma there was probably just one farmer whose mood this weather exactly suited, and that was Jesse Neighbours. He was spoiling for something, he himself did not know what. Now that he had nothing and no one to work for, he was working harder than ever, in the field before daybreak and out until after nightfall, unable to straighten his back, stalking down the rows (it was cotton-chopping time) with his hoe rising and falling as though motor-driven, neither speaking nor spoken to for twelve to fourteen hours at a stretch, so that his mind was furrowed by his thoughts as regular as a tractored field, throbbed to a beat as insistent as the rise and fall of his hoe. You chopped three acres a day and what did it get you? A plate of greens at night, enough to just keep you going tomorrow. You picked two hundred pounds, dragging the heavy sack after you like a wounded animal its entrails, bent double, blinded by your own salt sweat, no time to mop your brow, other hands quick to pick whatever you missed, half a cent a pound, take it or leave it, and at the end of the season what did you have? Enough to not quite pay your bill at the company store. Convinced now that farming was for fools—fools like him—Jesse delighted in every affliction that beset the crops: the fitful blossoming of the cotton, as if discouraged by the price it was fetching on the market, the coming of the boll weevils and the leaf hoppers and the corn smut, the blackbirds in clouds, the dust storms, the scorching sun that wrung a man out like a rag. He despised his condition and despised himself for acquiescing in it. And it was not long before that talk of desperadoes which had been dropped like refuse in a corner of his heated and airless brain burst aflame through spontaneous combustion.

People were robbing banks again, now that they had reopened following their little holiday. In town every Saturday there was talk of some bold new stickup. Then on Monday back to the fields, up and down the long weary rows, swinging a hoe or dragging a sack, and Jesse dreamed of fast cars, a new one stolen every week, always on the move, always in the money, spend it fast before it burned a hole in your pocket, plenty more where it came from, of living by the gun, quick on the trigger, feared and adored by multitudes, your exploits followed in the daily newspapers, good-looking women at your feet, fancy clothes, fast company. And when his name was on everybody's lips, then wouldn't Naomi feel sorry! Suppose you got caught? That was the risk you ran. Suppose you got killed? Suppose you did. Death by gunfire, quick, clean, a pistol bucking in your hand, at the end of a few glorious years, dying young and leaving a handsome corpse—compared with that was long life, spent in a cotton field, such a precious thing? Before long Jesse had begun to save up his money.

His earnings at picking went to the support of the family, but what he picked up playing Saturday-night dances was his. After being jilted he had recklessly gone back to smoking; now he quit again and once more began putting his tobacco money in a jar. It was no mule this time that he was saving for. He had to have a pistol; and before she would be reliable as a getaway car the old buggy needed a set of rings and at least one new tire to replace the one on the right rear with the boot and the slow leak around the valve.

Which bank Mr. O. B. Childress kept his money in Jesse did not know, but he wanted to be sure not to rob that one. Not that Jesse had any love for Bull. But Bull's money was, or would be, Naomi's; and if it should come to pass that having robbed just one bank and gotten away with it he decided not to make a career of it but came back home rich and they got married after all, he would not want it on his conscience that some part of his money was his wife's. The surest way to avoid it was to go outside the state.

Across the river over in Texas, in the county-seat town of Clarksville some forty miles away, was a bank which had been the object not long since of a spectacularly unsuccessful robbery attempt. The three robbers had been shot down like fish in a barrel as they emerged from the bank by lawmen posted on the adjacent rooftops. That gang had failed because they were too many—including a fourth who had informed the law of their plans. No one would be able to tip them off on him; and according to Jesse's calculations, swollen with self-conceit, the Clarksville sheriffs would be incapable of imagining that their bank might be struck again. And when things had blown over and he returned home in the chips, he would explain how he came into it by saying he had gone wildcatting in Texas and struck oil. And if he got caught? He was not aiming to get caught. And if he got killed? Who was there to care if he did?

The old buggy turned out to need more than a new tire or two, as Jesse found when, cotton picking over, he went to work on her. He gave her a valve job, up to his elbows in grinding compound, cleaned the plugs, put in points, regulated the timer. Then came the crowning touch, installation of a second carburetor, taken from the companion car, the adapter engineered by himself. The result: pickup that left new cars sitting, as he proved on the road to Tishomingo, where he went one day in October in quest of that pistol.

And on a subsequent trip shortly thereafter, thanks to those two carburetors, she hit seventy, shaking like a shimmy dancer, but she did it. That was a practice run down to Clarksville, where under an assumed name he opened a savings account at the bank with that fruit jar full of pennies and nickels and dimes, which took the teller a long time to sort out and count, giving Jesse a chance to study the layout.

He chose Halloween. You could wear a mask then and be just one among many, and the noise of firing, should it come to that, would be lost among the firecrackers and torpedoes. The night before Jesse wrote a letter to his folks, to be mailed from somewhere when the job was finished (it was found on him afterwards), explaining that he had left home to seek his fortune and would come back when he had made good, that he had left without saying goodbye so as to avoid tears, and not to worry about him.

He left the car in a side street in back of the bank, as planned, engine running, a thing that attracted no notice in those days when old cars were often left running at the curb for fear of their not starting again. In an alleyway he slipped on his witch's mask. The square was filled with masked revelers and there was noise of fireworks. At the door of the bank Jesse faltered for just a moment, then boldly stepped in.

It was all over in seconds. Jesse went to one of the cages, pulled his pistol, and said, "This is a stickup." The teller ducked, bells clanged, Jesse panicked and ran, straight into the arms of a bank guard, who held him in a bear hug while a second guard slugged him senseless with a blackjack.

A young man who identified himself as his attorney, appointed by the court, came round a few days later to visit Jesse in his cell. He was still new to his trade and nervous as a young intern with his first cancer patient. In exasperation he said at last, "Fool! If you just had to rob a bank, why didn't you pick one near home? Or don't you even know that here in Texas armed bank robbery is a capital offense?"

No, Jesse said, he never knew that.

At the trial the lawyer pled his client's youth and previous good character and lack of criminal record. But there had been a rash of bank robberies of late, and it was felt that an example must be made. Being from out of state went against the defendant also. The jury was out one hour and returned a verdict of guilty, and the judge sentenced Jesse Neighbours to die in the electric chair.

Appeal was denied, and in answer to their letter to the Governor of Texas Jesse's father and mother received a form reply regretting that nothing could be done, the law must take its course.

Execution was fixed for a day in February. Will and Vera went down to Huntsville the day before to bid the boy goodbye. They were given an hour together, but three quarters of it passed in silence. They spoke of things going on around home, as they had agreed beforehand they would. Once or twice they laughed over something, and once started all three laughed loudly. All through the interview his mother kept glancing nervously at her boy's hair despite herself, thinking of it being shaved off, as she had heard was done. Nothing was said about Naomi Childress. When the time was about up Jesse said he was sorry for the troubles he had brought on them, and they said not to think about that. He said tell his little brothers, and especially Doak, not to be proud of their outlaw brother and want to follow in his footsteps, but to be sensible boys and stick to farming, as crime did not pay. His mother would have liked to ask if he had made his peace with the Lord but was afraid of embarrassing him. When it came time to say goodbye they kissed and she managed to stay dry-eyed, as Will had admonished her that she must. It was he whose eyes filled with tears as he and Jesse shook hands.

They were told they could come for him anytime after seven the next morning. Money being a little tight, and neither of them feeling much like sleep, they passed the night sitting in the waiting room of the depot. They did not know the exact hour of execution. But when at shortly past five the lights in the station dimmed they reached for one another's hand and sat holding them until, after about four minutes by the clock on the wall, the lights brightened again. At seven at the penitentiary gate they found a truck waiting with a casket on the bed. They were given Jesse's effects, his guitar, his clothes, and a bale of tinfoil from the inner wrappings of ready-rolled cigarettes, each sheet rubbed out smooth as a mirror, at the sight of which his mother could not keep back a tear.

They were given a ride back to the depot in the cab of the truck. There the casket was put on the scales and weighed and Will paid the lading charges. Then it was put on a cart and rolled out to the end of the plaform. They went back to their seats in the waiting room. There remained in the shoe box which Vera had put up for their trip some biscuits and meat, but neither felt hungry. When the train came in they watched the casket loaded into a freight car. Their seats were in a coach in the rear. The overhead rack being too narrow for it, the guitar rode across their laps. And still though they sat, in four hundred and fifty miles it happened now and again that one or the other would brush the strings, drawing from them a low chord like a sob.

A
Good Indian

WHEN I WAS a boy I was ashamed of the color of my skin
—ashamed for my family, for the whole white race. From
that red Oklahoma earth which we walked upon and called
ours had sprung the red man; we palefaces were aliens and
usurpers. On our farm you could not plow ten feet, especially not after erosion had laid the soil bare and the dust
storms had flayed it rawer still, without turning up a
flint arrowhead, and while I treasured them, they were a
reproach to me. The name "Sooner," so proudly worn by
our state, to me was an emblem of infamy; and although
at school we were taught to glorify that day in 1889 when
our forefathers had gathered on the borders of what was
then called Indian Territory, poised themselves, and at
the crack of the starter's pistol swarmed in and staked their
claim to however much they could pace off and fence in,
I was not a bit proud of my grandfather's part in that ad-
venture. My father might sigh and say he wished Papa
had gotten more while the getting was good; to me it was
evident at an early age that Grandpa must have stolen our
fifty acres from some poor Indian brave, perhaps the very
one who, in leaving, had sown the earth with dragon's

teeth in the form of his arrowheads, and whom I pictured as proud and noble and sad, like the one on the head of the nickel.

Whenever I had a nickel, and bought myself a magazine, I sided with them—the Apaches, the Blackfeet, the Cheyennes—against my own people, and excused their cruelties. And when we kids played cowboys and Indians, I always took the part of Geronimo or Quanah Parker, and sometimes I came near to drawing blood with my stone tomahawk in trying to lift the scalp of my fallen paleface foe.

That tomahawk, by the way, was the genuine article. Like everybody else in our parts, we had an Indian burial mound on the property, and over the years ours yielded me, in addition to the tomahawk, stone grinding pestles and scraps of painted pottery, knucklebones, a skull, skinning knives of flint and obsidian, worn-down bits of antlers, and always arrowheads of all colors and of sizes for every variety of game, from tiny ones hardly bigger than a grain of corn, to great broadheads which I liked to think had once brought down two-ton buffaloes.

Feeling always something of a renegade (for stories of the Indian Wars were still told during my boyhood), I read all I could lay my hands on of the history of the Indians. The record of the white man's greed and perfidy was hardly to be believed. From the very beginning, in Jamestown and Massachusetts Bay, those original owners of the entire American continent welcomed the invaders as friends and neighbors, and where they did not make them outright gifts of land enough to live on (the Indians all had a very backward and undeveloped sense of individual land ownership and did not believe that one man could own what belonged to all men—what belonged, in fact, to no man, but instead to the Great Spirit), they sold it to them at fair, not to say overgenerous, prices. And then the whites

(I thought of them in those days as like white mice, with the quick, grasping paws and the sharp, busy teeth and the greedy little red bug-eyes of white mice) overran the Indians like a plague. In every state of the Union those who had once owned all saw it nibbled away and gobbled up until they were dispossessed of their ancient hunting grounds and herded into pens called reservations. Where they resisted they lost, and were punished for defending what was theirs. Where they conferred, and went voluntarily, with treaties guaranteeing the bounds of the reservation in perpetuity, they saw, in the same generation, in the same decade, often by the very signatories, every treaty mocked and broken. Mice do not know how to share; what's yours is theirs—all of it. And so the Indians were moved off these reservations to others farther west, on land belonging to yet other Indians, and given a treaty guaranteeing that it would never happen again.

Then positively the last resettlement was proposed—at gunpoint—to them. All the Indians, from all over, would be brought together in one large tract, and this land would be theirs for as long as the sun should shine: here was a treaty to show for it, hung with red ribbons and seals like tassels. And from the shrunken reservations which were all that remained to them of the land of their fathers, in Alabama, in Tennessee and Carolina and Mississippi and Florida, they were herded like winter cattle, and thousands left dead along the trail, to Oklahoma. It was not much good, this land; but it was theirs. The treaty was signed by the Great White Father in Washington, D.C. But Great White Fathers come and go, and that one was no sooner gone than the mice were running in the walls and boldly scampering out to thieve by night, and breeding and clamoring to get in; and the sun went down in the land which was to be theirs for so long as the sun should shine, and the red men were herded onto the last reservations, little pockets of the leanest land where the best was none too fat, and all the rest declared to belong to whichever white man got there "sooner" and staked his claim.

When you are a kid, you can get so carried away that those olden times seem more real to you than the times you live in.

I was scarcely able to look an Indian in the face whenever I met one on the street in town on a Saturday afternoon, when they came in from off the nearby reservation. I could scarcely believe they were Indians. They were parodies of white men, as a scarecrow is a parody of a man. Instead of beaded moccasins they wore broken-down old bluchers that the poorest poor white would long since have thrown away—possibly had. (I noticed the feet first, no doubt, because I hung my head and kept my eyes cast down.) Instead of fringed buckskin hunting shirts, they wore frayed and threadbare imitation-chamois workshirts, and over them wore baggy overalls of railway-engineer's pattern, black-and-white-striped. Instead of war bonnets of eagle feathers, they wore greasy old wool caps with pinched and broken bills or sweaty-banded old black felt hats with uncreased crowns. No bareback pinto ponies did they ride, but came in creaky old swaybacked wagons drawn by sway-backed mules with collar and trace galls and flyblown sores around their scrawny necks and down their slatted sides from pulling a plow. Along the tailgate of the wagon would sit a row of dark, runty children, stiff and impassive as a row of prize dolls in a carnival tent.

When, aged twelve, I accidentally opened our family skeleton cupboard one day and discovered hidden therein the fact that I myself had Indian blood, I at first did not know which to be, overjoyed or infuriated. I felt like the changeling prince in the storybook must have felt on discovering his true birthright, and discovering simultaneously that he had been done out of it, stolen and brought up by peasants as a peasant. I reproached my kin for having kept me in ignorance of this most important fact of my heritage. I begged for further knowledge. They seemed to know little and to care less. She was a Cherokee or a Choctaw, no one was sure which, and the man who had brought her into the family was dismissed as the squaw man. Possibly even she had been a half-breed (they seemed to prefer to think so), and so my share was only about one sixteenth, an amount to which most everybody in Oklahoma would probably have to own. Better just forget it, they said. Family matters, they seemed to be telling me, were best kept in the family. I vowed that when I grew up I would join a tribe and become an Indian.

Well, I grew up, all right, and in the process I lost my desire to become an Indian. Dirty pigs! My God, a white man may be poor, but if he's got any self-respect at all, he keeps himself clean, at least. They haven't got bathtubs? No running water? We never had, either. We toted the water in by the bucketful from the cistern, heated it in kettles and pots on the range, bathed in a number-three washtub on the kitchen floor. But we bathed. Every Saturday night. When we got done, and Mama got done reaming out our ears, and we stepped out, the water in that tub looked like blood, like a hog had been scraped in it, from that red Oklahoma dirt. We might have been poor, but we were always clean.

And poor as we were, we held on to our morals. We got pretty hungry, too; but we never stole, nor let our children thieve right out of the store bins in town. We'd have starved sooner than do that. And sooner than see our daughters and our sisters do what some of those Indian girls did for money, we'd have killed them first.

You can't help people that won't help themselves: that's

another thing I learned in growing up. You've got to have ambition. Whenever we got a dollar ahead, we didn't come into town with it and buy a quart of white lightning from some bootlegger in a back alley, get drunk and go crazy and start taking the place apart, wind up in jail with a head caved in from the constable's billy club, no use to ourselves or our families for the next thirty days. Indians just can't hold their liquor? In that case they ought to let it alone. I've heard it said they drink because they're downhearted. Because they've had it rough. Had a raw deal. We've all had it rough. We've all had a raw deal. But did we sit around moping about it forevermore? We bettered ourselves.

And just how rough did they have it when it was really rough all over? Living out there on the reservation all through '31, '32, '3, '4 on a steady government dole? Not much of a dole? Well, it was more than we got—and we paid taxes! They never had to worry that the bank was going to come around one day and say, "Well, Ed, old friend, you've been here a long time, and I hate to have to say it, but looks like you'll have to get off, you and your wife and kids." Best landlord in the world, good old Uncle Sam!

An Indian won't work. And don't give me none of that stuff about not having incentive. The answer to that argument is here: In 1935 a law was passed that the tribes could no longer hold the reservation lands in common (which is socialism) but it had to be divided up and parceled out among the members. The idea was to drag them into the twentieth century. Give them some incentive. Teach them what it means to a man to own his own little plot of ground, and to want to increase it, come up in the world. To weed out the freeloaders and give the real hustlers a chance to rise to the top of the heap. Did those lazy, good-for-nothing Indians work that land any harder when it was their own? They did not.

Now 1935, the year that law was passed, just happened
to be the year when oil was first brought in around our
section. I am not saying there was any connection; but once
each Indian owned his own piece of land he was free to
sell it if he had a mind to, not be told by the tribal council
that the land didn't belong to him, couldn't be traded. And
how do you suppose they spent the money they got for the
sale of their land? Well, I got my share. If they didn't have
any better sense than to spend it with me, that was their
lookout. They wanted what I had to sell, and if I hadn't
taken their money, there were plenty more who would have.

I had set up in business for myself in '33. I had the
local distributorship for Cadillac. As you can just imagine,
a man was not getting rich selling Cadillacs to Oklahoma
tenant farmers in 1933 and '4. But all of a sudden the
smart alecks who wouldn't let me in on the small family
cars just a year or so before were all laughing out of the
other sides of their mouths. For when a redneck who has
followed a plow all his life lays down the traces and picks
up a fortune in oil one day, he don't want him no Ford nor
Chevrolet, he wants him a *car*—the longest, fastest, gaudi-
est thing on wheels. And there was I, with just what he was
after. "The car you never thought you'd own"—that was
my motto.

I sold them with all accessories already on. Radio and
heater, chrome tailpipe, venetian blinds, seats upholstered
in leopard, zebra, spotted calf. The only thing that was
optional was the steer horns on the radiator grille. I stocked
Cadillacs in fire-engine red, oyster white, sky blue; but my
hottest number of all was a bile yellow that sharpened your
teeth like the smell of a sour pickle. That was the wagon
that really got the braves from off the reservation.

Some people—especially those on whose own farm-
steads one after another dry hole had been drilled—were
complaining in those days that the Indians had been given

all the oil-rich land. Others were not just sitting on their hands and howling, they were busy buying the redskins out. Some of those Indians sold out without even waiting for a drilling sample. Show them a few thousand dollars and that was all they needed to see—especially if they were seeing double. Others were told yes, no doubt about it, there was certainly oil lying under their land. But who knew how much? It might turn out to be a million barrels, and then again, it might not. It was a gamble, either way, but a bird in the hand . . . And there was I, or one of my men, before the ink on their X was dry—in line, I might add, with the Packard, the Buick, and the Pierce-Arrow dealers.

And then, a few months later, after they had run out of money to buy gas to put in them, or after they had driven them without any oil in the crankcase, you might see on a country road one of those Packards or Pierce-Arrows or Cadillacs hitched to a team of mules with the brave sitting on the hood on a blanket holding the reins, while inside, with the windows all rolled up regardless of the heat, sat the squaw and the papooses. Drive on a little farther down that same road, and you were apt to pass three or four more big-model automobiles upside down in the ditch or crumpled against telegraph poles.

But for running through cars, the Indian I am going to tell about holds the record.

One day one of my salesmen brought in a prospect known to everybody around town as John. If he had a second name, I had never heard it. John had sold out that very morning. Not being a very convivial sort, even in his cups, John had held out for and had gotten nine thousand dollars—plus a second bottle—out of the men who bought him out. He was a big buck with a face like a stone on the bottom of a creek, flat and featureless, and just as

36

full of smiles. Underneath his arm, the one without the
bottle, he carried a bundle wrapped in newspaper and tied
with twine, which I knew to recognize. They always in-
sisted on cash, and they wanted it always in ten-dollar bills,
possibly because those of larger denomination did not look
like money to them, and a ten really did.

Our demonstrator was one of those yellow dogs, and
my man had brought John in, at around eighty-five miles
per hour, in it. That was what he wanted, and he wanted it
now. I had sitting out back some three dozen jalopies and
homemade pickups cut down from old passenger sedans
and coupés and touring cars—Stars, Moons, and so help
me, one Marmon V-16. I had buggies, I had buckboards,
I had I don't know how many wagons, I had me about half
the mules in that county, for I'd seen booms before and I'd
seen busts, too, and I was hedging against the day when
they would need those wagons and teams again; I drew
the line only at travois. On this deal, though, I wasn't going
to have to take any trade-in.

I had on the showroom floor one exactly the same, but
no, John here wanted that demonstrator. She had a few
thousand miles on the speedometer, and I supposed he
wanted that particular car, thinking he would get a little
something off on the price. Little was what he would get,
all right; but I was prepared to powwow. However, John
did not want to bargain. He wanted that car the way he
might have wanted a particular woman for a squaw and
not her twin sister. He had seen what the one could do. I
took his parcel from him (this had to be done cautiously—
no sudden movements—like taking a bone from a dog),
untied the string, and counted out four hundred and twenty
ten-dollar bills. I told him that was what I wanted for my
automobile. John studied the stack I had made for a time,
then he stacked the rest alongside and studied the two of
them. After he had my car he would still have more money

than I would have. With a grunt, he pushed the smaller stack towards me. The bottle, too. To close the deal I had to drink with him.

While I was drawing up the bill of transfer, the salesman took the customer out for his driving lesson. This was a little service I offered, free of charge. They were gone about half an hour. When they returned, Doyle—Doyle Gilpin, my star salesman, himself part Kiowa—had a big purple knot over one eye. John X-ed the contract where I showed him to and I turned his ignition key over to him. I counted out to Doyle his commission, locked the money in the strongbox, locked the strongbox in the safe, and went to the show window to watch. The other salesmen, the parts-department man, and the mechanics from back in the shop all came out and joined us. These performances were always a sketch.

To see that Indian come up on that automobile was worth the price of a ticket. He carried the key hidden behind his back, as if it were a halter, and Doyle swore he was talking to that automobile under his breath all the while he sidled up to it, to coax it into standing still. Though he had been behind the wheel for his driving lesson, old habit was strong, and now he did not come at her from the driver's side because, unlike a white man, an Indian mounts a horse from the right. He stood stroking the door panel for a minute, then opened the door, saw he was on the off side, nodded to himself, shut the door, and, holding on to her all the while, made his way around the front end—never go behind them: that's where they can kick you.

"You say he claims to know how to drive?" I asked Doyle.

"Ugh," Doyle quoted.

It didn't look like it. He sat for the next five minutes

behind the wheel doing nothing at all. "Hellfire," I said, "he don't even know how to switch it on. Go out there and show—"

But John had known all along what to do; he had been just sitting there enjoying himself, like not wanting to put the match to a new brier pipe for savoring that never-to-be-recaptured moment of unused, fresh, factory-smelling ownership. The car John never thought he'd own for sure was his. They will tell you an Indian never smiles, but I have yet to see the one who doesn't when he switches on the ignition of his own new yellow Cadillac for the first time.

He put his foot on the accelerator and raced the motor up to where it sounded like a power saw, while we inside all winced. That was the one thing that used to bother me; I do hate to see a fine piece of machinery misused by falling into the wrong hands. Then he let out the clutch, or rather jerked his foot off of it, and away he went. He was right about that car: it bucked, it pitched, it snorted, it pawed, it leaped like—and in his hands, it was—a horse— an outlaw, a cayuse.

"Now you know," said Doyle, "how I got this bump on my head."

"Didn't you show him how to ease his foot off the clutch so as to keep that from happening?"

"Yeah, I showed him. He don't want to keep it from happening. That's the part he likes."

Now he rode her to earth. The gears meshed, and with a sound like satin ripping, he was off, discovering the horn in the process. And for the next hour he raced up and down Main Street, chasing pedestrians up onto the sidewalks, running up on them himself, slamming on his brakes, sitting on the horn, and letting the clutch out fast and bucking like a bronco. The town constable, with a little

39

urging from us car dealers, was not opposed to letting the boys enjoy themselves a little with their new cars, so long as nobody got hurt. There had been complaints about it in the beginning, just as the bankers had complained when pressure was put on them not to open accounts for the Indians; but just as the bankers came to realize that it was better for them as well to keep that money in circulation, so people generally came to realize that what was good for trade was good for the town as a whole. By about the time they had run through their complimentary three gallons of gas, the constable would tell them that was enough, and to go do their racing out on the country roads.

John, however, did not wait to be told. After a time he began to want company and tried to pick up a passenger, but nobody would ride with him. He invited Will Tall Corn, but Will just shook his head. Will's boy Henry was one of two friends to whom I had sold identical convertibles just a short while before, who, to settle a dispute the following week, ran them at one another head on from a distance of half a mile; that settled it, all right. Piqued that nobody would ride with him, John gunned out of town, going past my place and raising a cloud like a dust storm.

And that was the last we saw of him for about two hours, when, looking out the show window, I saw a wagon and team drawing up to the gas pumps, and driving them was John. I was showing a couple a car, but before those two made up their mind there would be three changes of model, so I turned them over to one of my assistants and went out.

"John!" I said. "Here, what's this? What have you done with that new car of yours?"

Well, it seemed that John's new car no go no more. John was disgusted with it. He seemed to expect me to give him that other one in replacement, the other yellow one. I said the warranty stopped just a little short of that, but let's have a look at his, chances were we could put it right if there was something the matter with it, get it going for him again. John, though, was really down on that car, never wanted to see it again, didn't even want to talk about it. Only very grudgingly did he consent to come with us in the wrecker and show us where he had left it.

What was keeping his car from going was a great big mean old tree in the way.

Taking notes on the scene were a couple of highway patrolmen, so while we towed in the wreck, John was taken down to the courthouse and charged with drunken driving, recklessness with an automobile, damage to public property (to get at the tree, he'd had to clip off a couple of the highway department's concrete fence posts), speeding, and if there had been such a thing as driver's licenses (there was later, of course, and it all but ruined the automobile business in Oklahoma for a time, especially the literacy test, but I wasn't hurt; on the contrary, I'd seen it coming and gotten out while the getting was good), why, I suppose they would have booked him for driving without any. As for the damage to his car, it looked a lot worse than it was. The front end was all smashed in, fenders and head lamps, bumper, grille, and the hood was sprung; but apart from the radiator and a bent fan and fan shaft, mechanically it was unharmed. For three hundred and fifty dollars —say five hundred—we could have it looking like new, almost.

But I never even got to quote him a figure before John started in again about wanting that other car, the one sitting on the showroom floor. His own, he refused even to come out and look at it. With that car John was finished. I was growing just a trifle impatient with trying to get it through that thick skull of his by sign language that cars weren't guaranteed against trees alongside the road, when John, pointing once again at the car on the floor, took from under his arm his parcel wrapped in newspaper, now considerably lightened, and put it in my hand.

It took me a minute to catch on, and when I did, I still didn't believe it. It's hard to credit foolishness, even when you've seen as much of it as I have. "You want to *buy* it, then?" I said. "Is that what you're saying? You want to *buy* that car?" There stood that savage without socks on his feet, wanting to buy his second Cadillac of the day!

What was more, he was ready to pay cash for it. No trade-in. He never even asked me to make him an offer on his other one. He could hardly wait for me to count the money. "Same," he said. "Same." Meaning it came to as much as he had paid for his first car.

"That may be," said I. "But the price ain't the same. This car here costs a little more than your other one. Because this one ain't never been rode by anybody, see?"

I figured he ought to have a good bit more money left than he had paid for his first car. That one had cost him forty-two hundred dollars, which, taken from nine thousand, left forty-eight hundred. Less twenty for wrecker service: forty-seven eighty. However, he had only forty-two hundred and eighty dollars on him. Where the other five hundred had gone didn't take three guesses. Fine or bail bond to those shysters down at the courthouse.

"Not enough," I said. Not caring particularly for the look on his face, I gave Doyle the sign, and he came over and joined us.

"I give you," said John, "my wagon and my team."

Not his other car. I'm slow, as I say, when it comes to taking in foolishness of that depth, but now it dawned on me that as far as John was concerned that other car of his was dead. Having no value to him any more, it had none that he could imagine for anybody else.

"I got me a wagon," I said. "I got mules."

"Good wagon," said John. "Good mules."

It wasn't a bad-looking team. Underfed, like all Indians' animals, but good stock. Not a bad-looking wagon, either.

"Wagons and teams not fetching much now," I said. "Everybody like you, wants a car. Nobody wants a wagon and team."

He just stood there, looking at me. I wondered what was going through that head. Nothing, it appeared.

Then Doyle spoke up and said, "How much does John need to have enough to buy him that yellow car?"

I said, figuring twenty-five dollars for the wagon and team and the harness, that would leave him still shy one hundred and fifty-two dollars and ninety-seven cents. "Make it a round hundred and fifty," I said.

"You don't suppose," said Doyle, "that we could allow John that for the wreck, do you? We ought to be able to strip a few spare parts off of it, oughtn't we?"

"Who are you working for," I said, pulling a sour face, "me or John?"

Then, with as good grace as I could, I gave in.

"Come see what our friend John has gone and done with his new car." It could not have been more than an hour later when Doyle Gilpin came in from giving a prospect a ride out in the country in our new demonstrator and said those words to me.

"Don't tell me," I said.

"Just come see," said Doyle.

I got up and followed. Doyle at the wheel, we drove out of town about five miles, being overtaken and passed by a siren car. We pulled up to where a line of cars alongside the road was already pulled up.

It was not a tree this time, it was a curve in the road,

43

and he must have tried to take it at no less than a hundred, for the car had finally come to rest a good fifty yards in the field beyond and must have turned over no fewer than half a dozen complete turns. Alongside the wreck, where the impact had thrown him, lay John—by old General Phil Sheridan's definition, a very good Indian.

There being no hospital in our town, thus no ambulance, the corpse was removed via pickup truck, to be left until called for by family or friends at the local funeral parlor.

The body gone, the crowd left. I stayed studying the wreck until all were gone. I would never have believed you could smash up a car to look like that.

"Nothing to do with that one," said Doyle, "but set a match to it."

It was just what I was thinking myself. No point in leaving an ugly sight like that to disfigure the beauty of the landscape, and to scare away trade.

"You got one on you?" I said.

"One what?" said Doyle.

I gave him a cigar, put one in my own mouth.

"One match," I said, waiting for a light.

And here now is the end of my story.

A little later in the day I was working at my desk when I had the feeling that somebody was watching me and looked up, and there standing in the doorway was this squaw. She was built like a sack of potatoes, and dressed like one, had a face the shape and the color of a deep-red potato. I hadn't heard her come in—you never do, they're as slinky as a cat and don't know that a door is for knocking on—but I felt she had been there for some time already before I noticed her, watching me out of those narrow, shiny black eyes.

44

"What can we do for you?" I said. For you never knew: tomorrow she might be a customer.

She never said anything.

I said, "It's around to the side there, if that's what's on your mind. Make yourself at home. It's free."

She just stood there, never batting a lash.

"Can't speak a word of English, I bet, can you?" I said. And I tried a couple of words on her which proved she couldn't. Can you just imagine it, a full-grown woman, born and brought up in the United States of America, and too lazy or too dumb or just too plained damned contrary to learn to speak the language? What are you going to do with people like that, I ask you.

Doyle Gilpin came in from the shop.

I said to Doyle, "Minnie Ha Ha here looks like she would like to use the Ladies'. Show her where to find it, will you?"

She and Doyle talked until it commenced to get on my nerves. It don't take much of that grunting and hawking to do it.

"What's all the palaver about?" I said.

"This here," said Doyle, "is Mrs. John. His squaw."

"Well? What does she want?" I said.

"She says, can she have back the wagon and team?"

"Oh, she does, does she? Well, would you please just explain to Mrs. John there that I took that wagon and team in on a trade on an automobile. And you might say that with things as they are I allowed about twice as much for it as it's worth."

More grunting, more hawking. "What's she jabbering about now?" I said.

"Says she needs it to take her man away in."

"Well, hell, lend her a wagon and a damned team. Let her have them two we took in on Monday. They ought to just about make it to the graveyard."

45

"She says she needs it to move with, too. She's got to get off the place tomorrow so they can start drilling for the oil."

"All right! Tell her she can borrow them for that too. Well, now what?"

"She says now that their land is gone, she ain't got no place to bury him in."

That was when I blew the whistle. "What in the infernal hell," I said, "has that got to do with me, I'd just like to know? Am I supposed to include a cemetery plot with every car one of these jokers buys from me?"

A Job
of the Plains

I

THERE WAS a man in the land of Oklahoma whose name
was Dobbs; and this man was blameless and upright, one
who feared God and turned away from evil. And there
were born to him three sons and four daughters. His substance also was one lank Jersey cow, a team of spavined
mules, one razorback hog, and eight or ten mongrel hound
pups. So that this man was about as well off as most
everybody else in eastern Pushmataha County.

Now there came a day when the sons of God came to
present themselves before the Lord, and Satan also came
among them. And the Lord said unto Satan, "Whence
comest thou?" Then Satan answered the Lord and said,
"From going to and fro in the earth and from walking up
and down in it." And the Lord said unto Satan, "Hast thou
considered my servant Dobbs, that there is none like him in
the earth, a blameless and upright man, one that fears
God and escheweth evil?" Then Satan answered the Lord
and said, "Does Dobbs fear God for nought? Hast Thou not
made an hedge about him, and about his house, and about

47

all that he hath on every side? Thou has blessed the work of his hands, and his substance is increased in the land. But put forth Thy hand now and touch all that he hath, and he will curse Thee to Thy face."

There was actually no hedge but only a single strand of barb wire about all that Chester Dobbs had. The Devil was right, though, in saying that the Lord had blessed the work of Dobbs's hands that year (1929) and his substance had increased in the land. There had been a bumper cotton crop, Dobbs had ginned five bales, and—the reverse of what you could generally count on when the crop was good —the price was staying up. In fact it was rising by the day; so that instead of selling as soon as his was ginned, Dobbs, like everybody else that fall, put his bales in storage and borrowed from the bank to live on in the meantime, and sat back to wait for the best moment. At this rate it looked as if he might at last begin paying something on the principal of the mortgage which his old daddy had left as Dobbs's legacy. And in fifteen or twenty years' time he would own a piece of paper giving him sole and undisputed right, so long as he paid the taxes, to break his back plowing those fifty acres of stiff red clay.

Then the Lord said unto Satan, "Behold, all that he hath is in your power. Only upon himself do not put forth thy hand." So Satan went forth out of the presence of the Lord.

"Well," said Dobbs, when those five fat bales he had ginned stood in the shed running up a storage bill and you couldn't give the damned stuff away that fall, "the Lord gives and the Lord takes away. I might've knowed it was too good to ever come true. I guess I ain't alone in this."

He had known bad years before—had hardly known anything else; and had instinctively protected himself

48

against too great a disappointment by never fully believing in his own high hopes. Like the fellow in the story, he was not going to get what he thought he would for his cotton, but then he never thought he would. So he borrowed some more from the bank, and butchered the hog, and on that, and on his wife's canning, they got through the winter.

But instead of things getting better the next spring they got worse. Times were so bad that a new and longer word was needed: they were in a depression. Cotton, that a man had plowed and sown and chopped and picked and ginned, was going at a price to make your codsack shrink, and the grocer in town from whom Dobbs had had credit for twenty years picked this of all times to announce that he would have to have cash from now on, and would he please settle his bill within thirty days? He hated to ask it, but they were in a depression. "Ain't I in it too?" asked Dobbs. What was the world coming to when cotton wasn't worth nothing to nobody? For when he made his annual spring trip to the loan department of the bank and was told that not only could they not advance him anything more, but that his outstanding note, due in ninety days, would not be renewed, and Dobbs offered as collateral the other two of his bales on which they did not already hold a lien, the bank manager all but laughed in his face and said, "Haven't you folks out in the country heard yet? We're in a depression."

Nevertheless, when the ground was dry enough that you could pull your foot out of it Dobbs plowed and planted more cotton. What else was a man to do? And though through the winter there had been many times when he thanked God for taking Ione's uterus after the birth of Emmagine, now he thanked Him for his big family. There was a range of just six years among them, one brace of twins being included in the number, and all were of an age to be of help around the place. The boys were broken to the plow, and the girls were learning, as plain girls did (might as well face it), to make up in the kitchen and around the house for what they lacked in looks. Levelheaded, affectionate, hard-working girls, the kind to really appreciate a home and make some man a good wife. And while boys went chasing after little dollfaces that couldn't boil water, they were left at home on the shelf. But, that's how it goes. Meanwhile they were a help to their mother. And when cotton-chopping time came they knew how to wield a hoe. And when cotton-picking time came all would pick.

Still, there were nine mouths to feed. Big husky hard-working boys who devoured a pan of biscuits with their eyes alone, and where were they to find work when men with families were standing idle on the street corners in town, and in the gang working on the highway you saw former storekeepers and even young beginning lawyers swinging picks and sledge hammers for a dollar a day and glad to get it? By night around the kitchen table the whole family shelled pecans with raw fingers; the earnings, after coal-oil for the lamp, would just about keep you in shoelaces, assuming you had shoes.

On top of this a dry spell set in that seemed like it would never break. In the ground that was like ashes the seed lay unsprouting. Finally enough of a sprinkle fell to bring them up, then the sun swooped down and singed the seedlings like pinfeathers on a fowl. Stock ponds dried up into scabs, wells went dry, folks were hauling drinking water. The boll weevils came. The corn bleached and the leaves hung limp and tattered with worm holes. The next year it was the same all over again only worse.

It got so bad at last a rainmaker was called in. He pitched his tent where the medicine shows were always held, built a big smoky bonfire, set off Roman candles, fire-crackers, sent up rubber balloons filled with gas and popped them with a .22 rifle, set out washtubs filled with ice water. Folks came from far and near to watch, stood around all day gawking at the sky and sunburning the roofs of their mouths, went home with a crick in their necks saying, I told you it'd never work. Church attendance picked up and the preachers prayed mightily for rain, but could not compete with the tent revivalist who came to town, pitched his tabernacle where the rainmaker had been, a real tongue-lasher who told them this drought was punishment for all their sins, bunch of whiskey drinkers and fornicators and dancers and picture-show-goers and non-keepers of the Sabbath and takers of the Lord's name in vain, and if they thought they'd seen the worst of it, just to wait, the good Lord had only been warming up on them so far. About this time word spread that on the second Tuesday in August the world was going to come to an end. Some folks pshawed but that Tuesday they took to their storm cellars the same as the rest. Towards milking time they began to poke their noses up, and felt pretty foolish finding the old world still there. The first ones up had a shivaree going around stomping on other folks' cellar doors and ringing cowbells and banging pots and pans. Afterwards when you threw it up to the fellow who'd told you, he said he'd got it from old So-and-so. Whoever started it nobody ever did find out.

One day the following spring an angel fell from heaven in the form of the county agricultural agent and landed at Dobbs's gate with the news that the government was ready to pay him, actually pay him, not to grow anything on twenty-five of his fifty acres.

What was the catch?

No catch. It was a new law, out of Washington. He didn't need to be told that cotton prices were down. Well, to raise them the government was taking this step to lower production. The old law of supply and demand. They would pay him as much not to grow anything on half of his land as he would have made off of the cotton off of it. It sounded too good to be true. Something for nothing? From the gov-

51

ernment? And if true then there was something about it that sounded, well, a trifle shady, underhanded. Besides, what would he do?

"What would you do?"

"Yes. If I was to leave half of my land standing idle what would I do with myself half the day?"

"Hell, set on your ass half the time. Hire yourself out."

"Hire myself out? Who'll be hiring if they all go cutting back their acreage fifty per cent?"

That was his problem. Now, did he have any spring shoats?

Did he! His old sow had farrowed like you never seen before. Thirteen she had throwed! Hungry as they all were, at hog-killing time this fall the Dobbses would have pigs to sell. And what pigs! Would he like to see them? Cross between Berkshire and razorback, with the lard of the one and the bacon of the other. Finest-looking litter of pigs you ever—well, see for yourself!

He had asked because the government was out to raise the price of pork, too, and would pay so and so much for every shoat not fattened for market. The government would buy them right now, pay him for them as if they were grown.

"Why? What's the government going to do with all them pigs?"

"Get shut of them. Shoot them."

"What are they doing with all that meat?"

"Getting shut of it. Getting it off the market. That's the idea. So prices can—"

"Just throwing it out, you mean? With people going hungry? Just take and throw it away? Good clean hog meat?"

"Now look a-here. What difference does it make to you what they do with them, as long as you get your money?

52

You won't have the feeding of them, and the ones you have left will be worth more."

"That ain't so good."

"How come it ain't?"

"The ones I have left I'll have to eat—the expensive ones. I won't be able to afford to eat them. Say, are you getting any takers on this offer?"

"Any takers! Why, man, you can't hardly buy a suckling pig these days, people are grabbing them up so, to sell to old Uncle Sam."

"No!"

"I'm telling you. And buying up cheap land on this other deal. Land you couldn't grow a bullnettle on if you tried, then getting paid not to grow nothing on it."

"What is the world coming to! Hmm. I reckon my land and me could both use a little rest. But taking money without working for it? Naw, sir, that sound I hear is my old daddy turning over in his grave. As for them shoats there, well, when the frost is in the air, in November, and I get to thinking of sausage meat and backbone with sweet potatoes and cracklin' bread, why then I can climb into a pen and stick a hog as well as the next fellow. Then it's me or that hog. But when it comes to shooting little suckling pigs, like drownding a litter of kittens, no sir, include me out. And if this is what voting straight Democratic all your life gets you, then next time around I'll go Republican, though God should strike me dead in my tracks at the polling booth!"

The next thing was, the winds began to blow and the dust to rise. Some mornings you didn't know whether to get out of bed or not. It came in through the cracks in the wall and the floor and gritted between your teeth every bite

53

you ate. You'd just better drop the reins and hightail it for home and the storm cellar the minute a breeze sprang up, because within five minutes more it was black as night and even if you could have stood to open your eyes you couldn't see to blow your nose. You tied a bandana over your face but still it felt like you had inhaled on a cigar. Within a month after the storms started you could no longer see out of your windowlights, they were frosted like the glass in a lawyer's office door, that was how hard the wind drove the dirt and the sand. Sometimes you holed up in the house for two or three days—nights, rather: there was no day—at a stretch. And when you had dug your way out, coughing, eyes stinging, and took a look around, you just felt like turning right around and going back in the house again. The corn lay flat, dry roots clutching the air. And the land, with the subsoil showing, looked red and raw as something skinned.

Then Faye, the oldest boy, who had been bringing in a little money finding day work in the countryside round-about, came home one afternoon and announced he'd signed up to join the Navy. Feeling guilty, he brought it out surlily. And it was a blow. But his father couldn't blame him. Poor boy, he couldn't stand any more, he wanted to get far away from all this, out to sea where there was neither dust nor dung, and where he might be sure of three square meals a day. Trouble always comes in pairs, and one night not long afterwards Faye's little brother, Dwight, too young to volunteer, was taken over in Antlers with a pair of buddies breaking into a diner. He was let off with a suspended sentence, but only after his father had spent an arm and a leg to pay the lawyer his fee.

Then the Dobbses went on relief. Standing on line with your friends, none of you able to look another in the face, to get your handout of cornmeal and a dab of lard, pinto beans, a slab of salt-white sowbelly. And first Ione, because being the mother she scrimped herself at table on the sly, then Chester, and pretty soon all of them commenced to break out on the wrists and the hands and around the ankles and up the arms and shins and around the waist with red spots, sores, the skin cracking open. Pellagra.

A man can take just so much. And squatting on the corner of the square in town on Saturday afternoon, without a nickel for a sack of Durham, without so much as a matchstick of his own to chew on, Dobbs said to his friends, "What's it all for, will somebody please tell me? What have I done to deserve this? I've worked hard all my life. I've always paid my bills. I've never diced nor gambled, never dranked, never chased after the women. I've always honored my old mama and daddy. I've done the best I could to provide for my wife and family, and tried to bring my children up decent and God-fearing. I've went to church regular. I've kept my nose out of other folkses' affairs and minded my own business. I've never knowingly done another man dirt. Whenever the hat was passed around to help out some poor woman left a widow with orphan children I've give what little I could. And what have I got to show for it? Look at me. Look at them hands. If I'd kicked over the traces and misbehaved myself I'd say, all right, I've had my fling and I've got caught and now I'm going to get what's coming to me, and I'd take my punishment like a man. But I ain't never once stepped out of line, not that I know of. So what's it all for, can any of yawl tell me? I'll be much obliged to you if you will."

"Well, just hang on awhile longer, Chester. Maybe them fellows will strike oil out there on your land," said Lyman Turley.

"Like they have on yourn," said Cecil Bates. "And mine."

"Lyman, you and me been friends a long time," said

Dobbs. "I never thought you would make fun of me when I was down and out."

"Hellfire, we're all in the same boat," said Lyman.

"What good does it do to bellyache?"

"None. Only how can you keep from it?" asked Dobbs. "And we're not all in the same boat. I know men and so do you, right here in this county, that are driving around in big-model automobiles and sit down every night of their lives to a Kansas City T-bone steak, and wouldn't give a poor man the time of day. Are they in the same boat?"

"Their day of reckoning will come," said O. J. Carter. "And on that same day, if you've been as good as you say you have, you'll get your reward. Don't you believe that the wicked are punished and the good rewarded?"

"Search me if I know what I believe any more. When I look around me and see little children that don't know right from wrong going naked and hungry, men ready and willing to do an honest day's work being driven to steal to keep from starving to death while other men get fat off of their misery, then I don't know what I believe any more."

"Well, you can't take it with you," said Cecil.

"I don't want to take it with me," said Dobbs. "I won't need it in the sweet by-and-by. I'd just like to have a little of it in the mean old here and now."

A breeze had sprung up, hot, like somebody blowing his breath in your face, and to the south the sky was rapidly darkening over.

"Looks like rain," said Cecil.

"Looks like something," said O.J.

"Well, men, yawl can sit here and jaw if you want to, and I hope it does you lots of good," said Lyman. "Me, I'm going to the wagon. I'd like to get home while I can still see to find my way there."

"I reckon that's what we better all of us do," said Dobbs.

The sky closed down like a lid. Smells sharpened, and

from off the low ceiling of clouds distant noises, such as the moan of a locomotive on the far horizon, the smoke from its stack bent down, broke startlingly close and clear. The telegraph wires along the road sagged with perching birds. They were in for something worse than just another dust storm.

To the southwest lightning began to flicker and thunder to growl. The breeze quickened and trees appeared to burst aflame as the leaves showed their undersides. Suddenly as the Dobbses came in sight of home the air was all sucked away, a vacuum fell, ears popped, lungs gasped for breath: it was as if they were drowning. Then the wind returned with a roar, and like the drops of a breaking wave, a peppering of hailstones fell, rattling in the wagonbed, bouncing off the mules' heads. A second wave followed, bigger, the size of marbles. Again silence, and the hailstones hissed and steamed on the hot dry soil. In the black cloud to the west a rent appeared, funnel-shaped, white, like smoke from a chimney by night, its point stationary, the cone gently fanning first this way then that way, as though stirred by contrary breezes. Shortly it began to blacken. Then it resembled a great gathering swarm of bees. Out of the sky fell leaves, straws, twigs, great hailstones, huge unnatural raindrops. The team balked, reared, began scrambling backwards.

"Cyclone!" Dobbs shouted. "Run for it, everybody! To the storm cellar!"

The boys helped their mother down the steps, pushed their sisters down, then tumbled in themselves while Dobbs stood holding the flapping door. He started down. As he was pulling the door shut upon his head there came an explosion. He thought at first they had been struck by lightning. Turning, he saw his house fly apart as though blown into splinters by a charge of dynamite. The chimney wobbled for a moment, then righted itself. Then the door was slammed down upon his head and Dobbs was entombed. Hands helped him to his feet. His head hit the low ceiling. He sat down on the bench beside a shivering body, a trembling cold wet hand clutched his. God's punishment for that wild talk of his, that was what this was. Dobbs reckoned he had it coming to him. He had brought it upon himself. He had also brought it upon his innocent family. Down in the dank and moldy darkness, where he could hear his wife and children panting but could not see their faces, and where overhead through the thick roof of sod he could hear the storm stamping its mighty feet, Dobbs sat alternately wishing he was dead and shivering with dread lest his impious wish be granted and his family left without support. Someone sobbed, one of the girls, and frightened by the sound of her own voice, began to wail.

In a husky voice Dobbs said, "Well now, everybody, here we all are, all together, safe and sound. Let's be thankful for that. Now to keep our spirits up let's sing a song. All together now, loud and clear. Ready?" And with him carrying the lead in his quavering nasal tenor, they sang:

> "Jesus loves me, this I know,
> For the Bible tells me so . . ."

II

AND THEN there is such a thing as foul-weather friends.

While people who had always been rather distant all went out of their way to be polite after oil was struck on Dobbs's land, all his old acquaintances avoided him. They had all come and bemoaned and comforted him over all the evil the Lord had brought on him, every man giving him a piece of money, taking in and housing the children, chipping in with old clothes after Dobbs's house was blown down; but as soon as his luck turned they would all cross over to the other side of the street to keep from meeting him. At home Dobbs grieved aloud over this. Good riddance, his daughters all said, and wondered that he should any longer want to keep up acquaintance with the Turleys and the Maynards and the Tatums, and other poor whites like that.

"The only difference between you and them pore whites is you ain't pore no more," said Dobbs. "Which you always was and very likely will be again. Especially if you talk thataway. Now just remember that, and meanwhile thank the Lord."

The girls clamored to leave the old farmstead and move into town. They wanted to live in the biggest house in town, the old Venable mansion, which along with what was left of the family heirlooms had been on the market for years to settle the estate. You could have pastured a milch cow on the front lawn, the grass so thick you walked on tiptoe for fear of muddying it with your feet. On the lawn stood a life-size cast-iron stag, silver balls on concrete pedestals, a croquet court, a goldfish pond with a water fountain. To tally all the windows in the house would have worn a lead pencil down to a stub. Turrets and towers and cupolas, round, square, and turnip-shaped, rose here, there, and everywhere; it looked like a town. You wanted to go round to the back door with your hat in your hand. Take a while to remember that it was yours.

At the housewarming it turned out that Dobbs and his daughters had invited two separate lists of guests, he by word of mouth, on street corners on Saturday afternoon, in the barber shop, hanging over fence gaps—they by printed invitation. Nobody much from either list showed up. First to arrive were their kin from the country, in pickup trucks and mule-drawn wagons and lurching jitneys alive with kids. The men in suits smelling of mothballs, red in the face from their starched, buttoned, tieless collars, wetted-down hair drying and starting to spring up like horses' manes, all crippled by pointed shoes, licking the cigars which Dobbs passed out up and down before raking matches across the seats of their britches and setting fire to them. The women in dresses printed in jungle flowers, their hair in tight marcelled waves against their skulls. The kids sliding down banisters, tearing through the halls, and skidding across the waxed parquet floors trying to catch and goose one another.

After them came a few of the many old friends and acquaintances Dobbs had invited. Then began to arrive the others, those who knew better than to bring their children, some with colored maids at home to mind them when the folks stepped out, people whom Dobbs had always tipped his hat to, little dreaming he would one day have them to his house, the biggest house in town, some of them the owners of the land on which his kin and the people he had invited sharecropped, so that quicker than cream from milk the two groups separated, he and his finding their way out to the kitchen and the back yard, leaving the girls and theirs to the parlor and the front porch. Then through the mist of pride and pleasure of seeing all those town folks under his roof, Dobbs saw what was going on. All of them laughing up their sleeves at the things they saw, passing remarks about his girls, who would take their part against him if he tried to tell them they were being made fun of by their fine new friends. Poor things, red with pleasure, stretching their long necks like a file of ganders so as to look a little less chinless, their topmost ribs showing like rubboards above the tops of their low-cut dresses. And his wife forgetting about the Negro maid and waiting on the guests herself, passing around the teacakes and the muffins, then getting a scorching look from one of the girls which she didn't understand but blushing to the roots of her thin hair and sitting down with her big red knobby hands trembling uselessly in her lap. Jumping up to say, "Oh, yawl ain't going already? Why, you just this minute come. Let me get yawl something good to eat. Maybe you'd like to try one of these here olives. Some folks like them. You have to mind out not to bite down on the seed." And through it all his old mama upstairs in her room, dipping snuff and spitting into her coffee can, refusing to budge, saying she didn't want to put him to shame before his high-falutin new friends, only he might send that sassy nigger wench up with a bite for her, just a dry crust of bread, whatever the guests left, not now, later, she didn't want to put nobody out.

Sightseeing parties were conducted through the house, the country kin making coarse jokes over the eight flush toilets which made his daughters choke red, though it was certainly not the first time they had heard the very same jokes. Others like Mr. Henry Blankenship saying, "What! Two hundred dollars for that rug? Oh, Chester, I'm afraid they saw you coming. Why oh why"—forgetting that until the day before yesterday they had never in their lives exchanged more than good afternoon—"didn't you come to me? I could have jewed them down fifty per cent at least."

The party broke up early, leaving mounds of favors; but not before each and every one of the relatives had gotten his corns stepped on. The townspeople went home sniggering with laughter, or fuming with outrage in the name of the vanished Venables. Both groups found excuses for declining future invitations, and in the evenings the big house on the hill heaved with sighs of boredom.

Dobbs continued as before to awake at four o'clock, and could not get back to sleep. The habit of a lifetime is not easily broken. But he could and did lie there smiling to think that he did not have to get up. No cow was waiting for him to milk her, no mule to be harnessed, no field to be plowed or picked of its cotton. Except that once awake Dobbs saw no point in not getting up. In fact, it bored him to lie in bed doing nothing. What was more, it seemed sinful.

He did not want to waste a moment of his leisure. Each day, all day, was his now, to spend as he pleased, according to his whim. Mere loafing was no pleasure to Dobbs; he had to be doing. The list of pastimes known to him was somewhat short. He went hunting with his fine new gun, went fishing with his bright new tackle, went driving in his big new car. One by one he slunk back to his old single-shot with the tape around the stock, with which he was a much better shot, back to his old cane pole, relieved to be rid of his level-wind reel which was always snarling in a knot and that boxful of artificial baits of which he never seemed to be using the right one. Fishing and hunting were not nearly so much fun when the time was not stolen from work. As he sat alone on the bank of a creek enjoying the blessings of unmixed leisure and telling himself how happy he was, Dobbs's hand would steal involuntarily to the nape of his neck where a welt, a rope burn which made it look like the neck of a hanged man, was, though fading now, still visible. It corresponded to the callus rubbed by the hames on the neck of a mule, and had been bitten there by plowlines, beginning at the age of eight. Dobbs rubbed it with a tenderness akin to nostalgia.

Other men were not to be found on the streets of town on a weekday; they were at work, and a lifetime of doing the same had left Dobbs with the feeling that it was wicked and immoral of him to be there at that hour. Those who were on the streets were those who were there at all hours, who often slept there: the town ne'er-do-wells and drunks.

Like all farmers, Dobbs had always lived for Saturday. That had been the day when he slipped the reins and came

62

into town. It was not the rest he enjoyed, though God knew
that was sweet, so much as the company. A man can plow
a field and plod along for five days at a stretch with nothing
to look at but the hind end of a mule and no company but
the cawing crows overhead, but then he has to see faces,
hear voices. Now that every day was a Saturday Dobbs
found himself looking forward to Saturday with a sense of
deliverance. But though they did their best to make him
welcome in his old spot, squatting among his cronies on
the square and whittling away the afternoon, his company
obviously embarrassed them. People he had always known
began to call him Mister, and many seemed to believe
that Dobbs thought they were no longer good enough for
him. People still said, as they had always done on taking
leave, "Well, yawl come," and Dobbs said it to them. He
meant it more sincerely with each passing day. But nobody
came and nobody was going to come. How could they drive
up that long raked gravel drive of his in a wagon and team
or a homemade pickup truck, traipse in their boots across
those pastures of carpet, come calling in overalls and poke
bonnets? And how could he draw up before their unhinged
gates and their dirt yards in that great long-nosed Pierce-
Arrow of his?

Three or four friends Dobbs lost forever by lending
them money and expecting them to pay it back. He supposed they felt he would never miss it, but he thought they
would despise themselves, as he would have, if they did
not repay him. And he lost more by refusing them loans.
Some people complained of the way he spent his money,
others of the way he hoarded it.

Which last, in fact, he had begun to do. Having done
nothing to deserve his sudden wealth, Dobbs feared it
might just as suddenly be taken from him. Being a wagon-
and-team man himself, he didn't much believe in oil, nor
in money which came from it. His bank statements fright-

ened him; he thought not how much he had, but how much it would be to lose! He developed a terror of being poor again. He knew what it was to be poor. So he told his children when they whined at him to buy them this and buy them that. Did they see him throwing money away?

True, he himself lived simply, indeed for a man in his position he lived like a beggar. But though he prided himself on his frugality, the truth was, and he knew it, that after a short while he found he simply did not like (he said he couldn't digest) filet mignon and oven-roasted beef and oysters and other unfamiliar and over-rich foods like those. After thirty years of Duke's Mixture he liked it, preferred it to ready-rolls. And cold greens and black-eyed peas and clabber: these were what he had always called food. Even they tasted less good to him now that he never worked up any appetite, now that they were never sauced with the uncertainty of whether there would be more of them for tomorrow. In fact, he just minced at his food now. Sometimes after dinner, as his girls had begun to call supper, and after everybody was in bed asleep, Dobbs would steal down to the kitchen, about half a mile from his bedroom, and make himself a glass of cornbread crumbled in sweetmilk or have some leftover cold mashed turnips, but he did not enjoy it and would leave it half finished. The Scriptures say, "Thou shalt eat thy bread in the sweat of thy face," and the sad truth is, to a man who always has, bread which does not taste of his own sweat just does not have any taste.

III

In all of Oklahoma no women were found so fair as the daughters of Dobbs; their father gave them equal inheritance among their brothers.

64

In his days of poverty the problem of marrying off his daughters had weighed on Dobbs's mind like a stone. He had felt beholden to them. For he had only to look in the mirror to see where they got their plainness from. But they were cheerful and uncomplaining, and when boys dressed in their best overalls and carrying bouquets went past their gate on Sunday afternoon as if past a nunnery, they had not seemed to mind. Now the problem was to keep them from marrying the first man who asked them. It was as if all four had come into heat simultaneously, and all day long and all night too, baying and snapping and snarling at one another, a pack of boys milled about the house and yard. They had given up all hope of ever catching a husband; now sweet words went to their heads like a virgin drink of spirits. "Don't you see that that rascal is just after your money?" Dobbs would say. And they would weep and pout and storm and say, "You mean you're afraid he's after your old money. That's all you ever think about. You don't know Spencer like I do. He loves me! I know he does. He would marry me if I was poor as a churchmouse. He told me so. If you send him away you'll break my heart and I'll hate you till the day I die."

Dobbs even had to buy off one of them. One of the suitors, that is. Pay him to stay away, keep him on a regular monthly salary.

So inflamed did poor Denise get that she eloped with a fellow. Dobbs caught them in Tulsa and brought her home fainting and kicking and screaming. Even after it had been proved to her that he was wanted for passing bad checks from Atlanta to Albuquerque, she still sulked and went on pining for her Everett. The twins, who before had always gotten along together like two drops of water, now decided they each wanted the same boy, though Lord knew there were plenty to go around, and they only patched up their quarrel by turning on their father when he said that only

65

over his dead body would either of them marry that no-good fortune-hunting drugstore cowboy.

One by one they beat him down. For Denise another Everett came along and she told her father she meant to have this one. The old refrain: he's only after your money. "I'm free, white, and twenty-one," she said, "and seeing as it's my money, I'll spend it on what I please." Dobbs shook his head and said, "Oh, my poor girl, my poor little girl, you're buying yourself a bushel of heartache." She replied, "Nonsense. If this one don't work out to suit me I'll get shut of him and get me another one." And that in fact was how it did work out, not once but four times.

She had the biggest wedding the town had ever seen. Dobbs spared no expense. At the wedding reception in his own house he was a stranger; he knew no one there. Then the twins were married in a lavish double ceremony. People said you couldn't tell the girls apart; what Dobbs couldn't tell one from the other were their two husbands. Emmagine was not long behind them, and her wedding put theirs in the shade, for she had married a Lubbock of the Oklahoma City Lubbocks. This time there were two wedding receptions, one at Dobbs's, the other at the home of his son-in-law's people. Dobbs attended only the one, though he paid the bills for both. In fact, the day after the ceremony he began to receive unpaid bills from his son-in-law's creditors, some dated as far back as ten years.

Then Ernest, the middle boy, brought home a bride. Mickey her name was. She had hair like cotton candy, wore fishnet stockings, bathed in perfume. Thinking she might have caught cold from going around so lightly dressed, Mrs. Dobbs recommended a cure for her quinsy. But there was nothing the matter with her throat; that was her natural speaking voice. She and her sisters-in-law backed off at each other like cats. The family seldom saw Ernest after he left home. The checks his father sent him came back cashed by banks in faraway places. He wrote that he was interested in many schemes; he was always on the verge of a really big deal. To swing it he needed just this amount of cash. When he returned once every year to discuss finances with his father he came alone. His mother hinted that she would have liked to see her daughter-in-law and her grandson; as luck would have it, one or the other was always not feeling up to the trip. Once the boy was sent alone to spend a month with his grandparents. Instead of one month he was left for four. To his shame Dobbs was glad to see the boy go. When Ernest came to fetch him home he took the occasion to ask for an increase in his allowance. He and his brother quarreled; thereafter he stayed away from home for even longer stretches.

Back from his hitch in the Navy, and back from his last cruise parched with thirst and rutting like a goat, came Faye. Feeling beholden to the boy for the hard life he had had on the farm and on shipboard, Dobbs lavished money on him. When he was brought home drunk and unconscious, battered and bruised from some barroom brawl, Dobbs held his tongue. To hints that he think of his future he turned deaf. The contempt he felt for work was shown in the foul nicknames he had for men who practiced each and every trade and profession. Once to Dobbs's house came a poor young girl, obviously pregnant. She claimed the child was Faye's. He hardly bothered to deny it. When his father asked if he meant to marry the girl he snorted with laughter. He suggested that she would be happy to be bought off. Shrinking with shame, Dobbs offered her money; when she took it he felt ashamed of the whole human race. He told his son that he was breaking his mother's heart. He said there would always be money to support him but that it was time he settled down and took a wife. The one he got persuaded him that while he was away in the Navy his sisters and brothers had connived to cheat him of his share of the money. He had been cheated of something, he somehow felt; maybe that was it. To have a little peace of mind, his father gave him more; whatever the amount, Faye always felt sure it was less than he had coming to him. He quarreled with his sisters. Family reunions, rare at best, grew more and more infrequent because of the bad feelings between the children.

It was Dwight, his youngest son and always his favorite child, on whom his father placed his hopes. Totally reformed after that one scrape with the law, he never drank, never even smoked, never went near a poolhall nor a honkytonk. Most important of all, girls did not interest him in the least. He was in love with the internal combustion engine. His time was spent hanging around garages, stock-car race tracks, out at the local cowpasture with the windsock and the disused haybarn which was hopefully spoken of as the hangar. He worshipped indiscriminately automobiles, motorcycles, airplanes, whatever was driven by gasoline. The smell of hot lubricating oil intoxicated him. Exhaust fumes were his native air. Silence and sitting still drove him distracted. He loved having to shout above the roar of motors. He spoke a language which his father could only marvel at, as if he had raised a child who had mastered a foreign tongue, speaking of valve compression ratio, torque, drop-head suspension, and of little else.

Dwight had known the ache, the hopeless adoration worlds removed from envy, too humble even to be called longing, of the plowboy for cars that pass the field, stopping the mule at the sound of the approaching motor and gazing trancelike long after it has disappeared in a swirl of dust, then awakening and resettling the reins about his neck and pointing the plowshare down again and saying to the mule, "Come up, mule." Now he saw no reason why he shouldn't have one of his own. He was sixteen years old and his old man had money to burn. Car or motorcycle, he would have settled for either; the mere mention of a motorcycle scared his father into buying him a car. He was not going to kill himself on one of them damned motorsickles, Dobbs said, words which just two months later came back to haunt him for the rest of his life.

It was a Ford, one of the new V-8's. No sooner was it bought than it disappeared from sight. He was working on it, said Dwight. Working on it? A brand-new car? If something was the matter with it why not take it back? All that was the matter with it was that it was a Detroit car, off the assembly line. He was improving it.

"You call that improving it!" said Dobbs on seeing it rolled out of the old Venable coach house a week later. It looked as if it had been wrecked. The body all stripped down. The entrails hanging out of the hood. Paint job spoilt, flames painted sweeping back from the nose and along the side panels in tongues of red, orange, and yellow. Dwight said he had added a supercharger, a second carburetor, advanced the timer, stripped the rear end. Well, just drive careful, that's all. Two months later the boy was brought home dead. Coming home from the funeral Dobbs's wife said, "This would never happened if we had stayed down on the farm where we belonged. Sometimes I wish we had never struck oil."

The same thought had crossed Dobbs's mind, frightening him with its ingratitude. "Ssh!" he said. "Don't talk like that."

With the death of Dwight, Dobbs and his wife were left alone in the big house with only Dobbs's old mother for company. She threatened to leave with every breath. She could see well enough where she wasn't wanted. She would not be a burden. If she wasn't good enough for her own flesh and blood just say so and she would pack her bag. The visits home of Faye and Ernest all but ceased. As for the girls, they were never mentioned. Both Dobbs and his wife knew that they were ashamed of their parents.

And so the Lord blessed the latter end of Dobbs more than his beginning. For in addition to his oil wells, he had (he never did come to trust oil, and old country boy that he was, converted much of it into livestock) fourteen thousand head of whiteface cattle and five thousand Poland China hogs.

He also had two sons and four daughters. And he gave them equal inheritance, though there was not one who didn't believe that the rest had all been favored over him.

After this lived Dobbs not very long. Just long enough to see his sons' sons, and despair.

So Dobbs died, being old before his time, and having had his fill of days.

Mouth
of Brass

"MOLLY OT! Hot tamales!"

Down from the top of our street each weekday after-noon that cry, in a voice deeper than any I have ever heard in all the years since, used to come rumbling like thunder.

"Finus! Here comes Finus!" I would run shouting to my mother.

Shaking her head, my mother would declare, "Boy, you're going to ruin your digestion eating those things. Going to just burn the lining of your insides right out. Wait and see." However, she always ended by saying, "All right. Go find me my purse." For it was true, hot spices kept a child purged of worms. And often instead of a nickel my mother would give me a dime, saying, "Might as well get me a couple too while you're at it." They were so delicious the way Finus made them that afterwards we used to suck dry the cornshucks they came wrapped in.

Meanwhile his cry, nearer now, would roll out again, sonorous as a chord drawn from the deepest pipes of a church organ. And if outside our house he should loose

71

another, the chimes of our doorbell shuddered softly and teacups rattled on their saucers.

No matter what Finus said it came out sounding proud and mighty; so he said as little as he could without risk of seeming impolite. In another place, or at some later period perhaps, his voice might have made Finus's fortune; but in Blossom Prairie, in east Texas, in 1930, to be answered by a Negro in that powerful bass brought the blood to some men's cheeks quick as a slap. His size alone was a standing challenge, the silence in which he took refuge easily misinterpreted as surliness; add to these provocations the sound that came out of him whenever he did speak, and Finus was often in trouble of the kind I myself had witnessed one Saturday afternoon on the town square when a sailor knocked him down, saying, "I'll teach you to talk back to a white man in that tone of voice." From where he lay amid the cornshucks from his tamales strewn on the pavement Finus said, and the weariness of his tone deepened it further still, "I speak to everybody in the voice God give me." He was born loud as surely as he was born black: his name will tell us so. For although he was called, and called himself, Finus, to rhyme with minus, this is doubtless a corruption of Phineas, and that, as someone knew who heard the infant utter his first wail, means in Hebrew "mouth of brass."

II

HIS LAST NAME was Watson, though there were probably not a dozen people in Blossom Prairie who ever knew it, despite the fact that he had been there long enough to have become a fixture of the place. To sell his hot tamales "Finus" sufficed him. He made his daily rounds and cried his wares; otherwise, being black, he passed unnoticed, except from time to time when somebody, most often a man from out in the country, unused to our stentorian Negro, took exception to his attitude—mistaking his voice for his attitude.

He lived all alone in a shanty down behind the Catholic church, across town from the section along the creek north of the jailhouse where the other Negroes all lived. There in a series of old packing crates Finus raised the chickens that went into his hot tamales, and on a small plot of ground grew the red peppers and the herbs with which they were seasoned. He was said to have Mexican blood, and in a certain light could be seen a dark gleam on his high cheekbones as of copper beneath a coat of soot. To this drop of Mexican in him was attributed his independence—his "impudence," some called it—the reserve with which he held himself aloof from the other Negroes of the place, and the flavor of his tamales, the inimitable tang of his barbecue sauce. This last he produced at Fourth of July celebrations, for which he was always in demand as cook, and on Juneteenth—June the nineteenth, observed by our Negroes as the day in 1863 when, six months late, news of the Emancipation Proclamation reached Texas. At the time I first knew him Finus was in his late forties or early fifties—long a familiar figure in my home town. Into every quarter of it his fixed round brought him daily, Saturdays and Sundays excepted; and it was said that so punctual was his appearance in each of the streets along his route the people there all set their clocks by the sound of his booming voice.

Our street, which he reached just at four, lay towards the end of Finus's route. After he and I became friends I used to meet him at the top of our street every afternoon and he would give me a ride down to my house on the lid of his box, which hung by a strap from his shoulder. This box was a marvel of Finus's own making. Sitting on it one

73

felt no heat at all, but when it was opened heat burst from it as from an oven. An oven, in fact, it was: inside it burnt a smokeless charcoal fire, and on cold days when Finus raised the lid he would be momentarily enveloped in a cloud of spicy steam.

When Finus knelt and opened his box to sell me my tamales I could see that it was nearly empty. Yes, he said, he was heading for home now. But in the morning when he set out, his box was full to the top—too heavy for him to give a boy a ride on it. I questioned him about his route, and when he told me he went as far as the ice house and the railway depot, the cotton compress and the courthouse, that he crossed the public square not once but four times every day, I listened in wonder and longing, as one who has never left home listens to the tales of a traveler. I had myself seen those same sights, to be sure; but usually from a back window of the car, and even so, not very many times.

"How would you like to come with me one day?" asked Finus.

I knew that "one day." It meant when you are big. It meant never.

But not when Finus said it. "All right, you ask your mama," he said. "If she says you can go, then you pick the day and I'll take you with me."

I started to ask my mother at once, as soon as Finus had set me down at our door. But I checked myself. I feared that should she say no Finus might take it as a rebuff. Instead I waited until I heard his voice come up from below as, turning the corner, he proclaimed his advent in the next street.

"Well, wasn't that nice of Finus," said my mother. But before saying whether or not I could accept his invitation she would first have to talk it over with my father. I coaxed from her a promise to speak to him that evening. In bed that night I awaited his decision anxiously. I sensed in my father a reservation about my friendship with Finus. It was not that he frowned at it exactly; he seemed rather to smile at it somehow. When my mother came to kiss me goodnight she said I could go. When I told Finus the following afternoon he proposed that we make it the very next day. What was more, I was to come early to his place and help him make his tamales.

III

IF I SHOULD tire out and become a burden on him he was to leave me off at my father's shop on one of our trips through the square: with this parting instruction to Finus my mother left me in his care and drove away. I experienced a moment's homesickness then and wished I had not come.

I had never been inside a Negro's house before, and through the dark opening of Finus's doorway I passed as through a wall. The house consisted of just one room, most of it devoted to the manufacture of hot tamales. A big black cast-iron wood range, heavily scrolled and garlanded, squatted on its paws against one wall. In the center of the room stood a long wooden table, its top as scarred as a butcher's block and bleached colorless from scrubbing, on which was heaped a mound of finely shredded cooked chicken meat. From nails on the walls hung clusters of dried and shriveled red peppers and bunches of dried herbs. In one corner stood Finus's cot. Beside it stood a washstand on which sat a basin and ewer. The bare simplicity of Finus's way of living made it seem to me like play, and this combined with my sense of strangeness at being inside a Negro's house to remind me of the time I had timidly knocked at the door of a clubhouse built of scrap lumber and belonging to a gang of older boys and had snatched one tantalizing glimpse of the snug interior before being told that members only were allowed inside, scram! Finus's house was like but better than that clubhouse, and I had been invited in.

The chickens for his hot tamales, Finus explained, were always killed and partly cooked the night before. Now into one of the two huge caldrons steaming on the range he emptied a sack of cornmeal. In with the meal then went the meat, stirred in with an ax handle which from long usage had been boiled white as a bone. Into the other caldron went an armload of dry cornshucks. For poking these down so that more could be added as they softened in the hot water Finus had another ax handle, like the first whitened by boiling. After the meat and the mush had cooked together for a while Finus opened a large jar filled with a red powder and poured in about half the contents, and the air of the room sharpened suddenly with the odor of hot chili peppers.

Then the limp wet shucks were spread out in rows on the tabletop like a game of solitaire and the pot of mush brought steaming to the table. A spoonful of it on a shuck, a lengthwise roll, a fold at each end: and there you were. Between us we made two hundred hot tamales. I made three and Finus made the other hundred and ninety-seven. Next to his mine looked like roll-your-own cigarettes next to ready-rolls. I was promised my three for my dinner. Two hundred hot tamales on weekdays, twice as many on Saturdays . . . somebody had once worked it out for him, and it came to nearly two million tamales that Finus had made in his time. And while chicken feed had gone up to two dollars a sack and cornmeal to four dollars a barrel, he still charged the same as always: "Two for a nickel, two bits a dozen!"

76

IV

ACTUALLY to be making his rounds with him when Finus rumbled "Molly ot! Hot tamales!" filled me with such pride that my face ached from grinning.

"Got yourself a helper today, I see, Finus," said housewives who came out to buy from us.

"Yes, ma'am, that's right, I've taken me on a partner here," Finus solemnly replied; and I observed that even when Finus meant to agree, and repeated what had been said to him, his voice made it sound rather as though he were correcting the person.

When children came to buy and Finus let me fill their orders from out of his box and collect their nickels I swelled so with self-importance I could scarcely contain myself. And the best was yet to come. Before we had gone far, just as we were entering a new street, Finus said, "You want to holler 'Hot tamales'? Go ahead." I nearly tore my lungs loose trying to make it sound loud and grand like Finus's cry. Thereafter, for as long as my voice held out, sometimes I hollered, sometimes Finus, sometimes we hollered both together. It must have sounded like a tuba accompanied by a piccolo.

Certain streets down which we went I knew, or I recognized as those on which lived playmates of mine to whose houses I had been brought to spend an afternoon. Other streets were entirely new to me, and leading off these were dozens more. I wondered how people could speak of our town as a small town. Finus, who knew it better than anyone else, who traversed its length and breadth daily, estimated it to be five miles long east to west, only a little less north to south. That was plenty big enough, we agreed. It was the county seat, with a population of three thousand. A person could live there and believe just about any-

77

thing and find somebody to agree with him—and a lot more to disagree with him: there were (Finus had counted them) nineteen churches, white and colored, scattered around town. The dog population Finus put at eight hundred and seventy, most of them known to him personally by name.

We crossed the square for the first time and went out by the street running behind the post office. This brought us to the cotton compress and the cottonseed mill, which always smelled so good. There we turned and went skirting along the railroad tracks until we came to the depot. We came back down Depot Street, then turned into Negrotown, where the paved streets gave out and became dirt streets. Clotis, who did our wash, came out and bought half a dozen tamales from me. We came out between the courthouse and the jail, crossed Market Square, and passed through the public square for the second time. Finus asked was I tired and would I like to stop and stay with my father. I spurned the suggestion and we continued on.

It pleased Finus to stop and ask, "Know where you're at now?" I would have to say no. Shortly I began, so great was my pleasure in this game, so confident was I of the next turn it would take, almost to shout with glee, "No! Where, Finus?" For when he had turned me around and around and had me completely lost, precisely then would Finus take my hand in his, lead me around a corner, and there we were before some dear familiar landmark of the town: the courthouse tower, the steeple of one of the churches, one of the bridges over the creek, or most frequently, and always with the greatest surprise, the keenest joy, the bright, busy square, heart and center of my world, scene of my Saturdays.

I began that day to acquire a sense of the relation of these places one to another, of the overall plan of my town. As in those puzzles in which one draws lines between dots until suddenly a recognizable creature or object emerges, I was drawing lines between what before had been disconnected dots forming no pattern or design. It was doubly delightful because it was both new and familiar.

Nor could I, in getting to know my fellow townsmen, have found a better guide than my friend Finus, the hot-tamale vendor. Cliff Allen, the livery-stable owner; Mr. Kirkup, the blacksmith; Mr. Green, the garage mechanic; the firemen at the firehouse: all the most interesting people liked hot tamales. Even among the housewives the ones who came to their doors in answer to Finus's cry were those unsoured by dyspepsia, the jolly young spice-loving ones. In Market Square the farmers at their wagons bought from us, and the prisoners in the jailhouse, hearing our cry, called down from their barred windows and sent the deputy sheriff, a handsome, stern-looking man with a stag-handled pistol in a holster on his hip, out to buy theirs for them.

When Finus, having ridden me down on the lid of his box from the top of our street, as usual, set me down at my door that afternoon, exhausted, hoarse from yelling, and deliciously happy, I was a different boy from the one who had left home only that morning. The world had been revealed to me much bigger and much more exciting than I had dreamed. With much of it I was now acquainted, much of it I had yet to explore. For both this knowledge and this promise I had Finus to thank, and as I heard his voice swell up from the bottom of the street my heart swelled with gratitude and affection for my friend, my guide.

V

ON SATURDAYS, as I have said, Finus did not make his rounds; instead he stood with his box, or rather two boxes, on the northwest corner of the square, lifting his cry from time to time above the din. For in Blossom Prairie nobody stayed at home on Saturday unless forced to; all who could possibly get there spent the day downtown. The population doubled—in ginning season tripled—as country folks poured in by the car, the truck, and the wagonload. The square was a carnival. The storefronts were decked with streamers offering prizes and free toys. From the open window of its projection room, above the whirr of the machine, the picture-show discharged the thump of the overture to *William Tell* and *The Flight of the Bumblebee,* and laid down along the sidewalk beneath the marquee the odors of hot buttered popcorn and heated celluloid. Children out of school with their allowances burning their hands and grownups with their weekly paychecks in their pockets thronged the walks, window-gazing. All the air was spiced with the odors of holiday foods from the busy cafés, the confectionery, the street vendors, like my friend Finus, of hot tamales and hotdogs, parched peanuts, doughnuts, watermelon. Town folks met their country kin on the square that day, and country folks met their friends from other parts of the county. In the evening after work and after an early supper families drove down and parked their cars against the curbs and watched the promenaders stroll past, took a few turns themselves; then the men gathered for talk on the corners, the children played games around the Confederate monument in the center plaza, and the women exchanged visits with one another in the cars.

From the time I was born I was taken regularly each week to join that festive crowd; but not until after my tour of the town with Finus, and then not at once but only after much wheedling, did my mother consent to let me go down on the square "all by myself." When she did I felt I could begin to think of myself as a big boy, though still a dozen *dont's*—enough to make a person wonder whether the world was a safe place to live in—were repeated to me each time I set off from home, the one above all being not to go into any of the alleyways that enclosed the square like a moat on four sides. It was in their shadowy depths, at the back doors of the domino parlors and the poolhalls and the cafés, that the bootleg whiskey flowed on Saturdays, the dice games were played, the fistfights fought. But I am getting ahead of myself. Of that side of life in my home town I knew nothing until one day in my tenth year. After that nothing was ever the same for me again.

Say that the first scene I saw was at four o'clock in the afternoon, then the drama began at three fifty-five when from out of one of those back alleys where he had drunk too much whiskey and gambled away too much money this Jewel Purdom returned to his car parked against the south-side curb to find his young though already large brood quarrelsome and hungry and sent one of them, his boy Gilbert, across the square to buy a dozen of Finus's hot tamales.

Afterwards nobody could be found who had seen the boy make his purchase. Nobody could be found who had seen anything of all that happened, despite the fact that it was a Saturday in early fall when crops were in and farmers idle and with money for their wives to spend and on all four corners of the square the crowds stood elbow to elbow. I was playing around the monument in the plaza at the time; however, I can relate how it went as surely as if I had been present on the spot, for Finus had a little routine with children: I have seen it many times and it never varied.

"Put your hands together and hold them like this," he

always said, kneeling and putting his hands together, the polished yellow palms opened upwards. Upon the child's hands he laid a pad of three or four sheets of newspaper. He then raised the lid of his box, releasing that mouth-watering aroma. When the child was one the age of Gilbert Purdom, Finus gave him a lesson in how to count, speaking the numbers slowly and enunciating with ponderous care in that deep voice of his and encouraging the child to repeat after him as with his tongs he stacked the tamales on the paper. "And twelve makes a dozen," he concluded. Then he added one more.

Gilbert Purdom thought when he was given that extra hot tamale that he was getting preferential treatment. He did not know that Finus always gave thirteen to the dozen. He reasoned that his father and mother and his brothers and sisters were not expecting an extra free tamale either. So as soon as he had gotten among the crowd Gilbert popped that tamale in his mouth. It went down so quick that before he knew it he had eaten another. Gilbert may have been surprised then but he was not alarmed. He had that one coming to him. The first one nobody would know to miss, the second one was his share. What did it matter when he chose to eat it, now or together with the family? Still, Gilbert quickened his pace so as to put temptation behind him. But in front of him, right under his nose, Gilbert had eleven spicy hot tamales—or rather, ten. And now as he dodged among the crowd Gilbert's short thin legs were pumping as fast as he could urge them and he was panting, not so much from exertion as from fear—fear of the devil that had gotten into him.

Gilbert was across the square and back at the car within two minutes after leaving Finus. Yet all he got back with were eight tamales. And already Gilbert was beginning to wish he had not done what he had done for more reasons than one.

Gilbert had not thought up any trick to save himself from the resentment of his brothers and sisters and the anger of his father. He had not had time to think. Besides, his crime was so gross that he despaired of escaping punishment. He had given himself up for lost with the eating of that third tamale. So as not to add insult to injury he had wiped the grease off his mouth, but he did not even attempt an alibi, just held out the package with a blank look on his face that passed for innocence. Gilbert would have lied, though he knew the truth was bound to come out sooner or later, for by then he was as heedless of the consequences of being caught in a lie as he was of being caught stealing when that fourth tamale, now beginning to cause him such different sensations, was just melting in his mouth; only he could not think of any lie. What saved Gilbert was not native cunning or sudden inspiration, it was sheer luck. It was his father's saying, "Is these here all that nigger give you for your money?"

I was to see the Purdoms father and son on the square on Saturday afternoon many times in after years—I would once even see Jewel Purdom lounging against the wall of the bank in the very spot that had once been Finus's old spot; but I heard the name and saw them both for the first time to my knowledge that day; saw them twice. The first time was when, sitting on the curb of the plaza resting from my game of tag, I saw this man stalk past carrying a package wrapped in greasy newspaper and dragging this little boy by the hand. The looks on their faces made me say to myself, "Uh-oh. There's a boy who's fixing to get a whipping." Not that I felt very sorry for that boy, even so.

The second time I saw the Purdoms was less than five minutes later. I was still catching my breath, still sitting in the same spot, when they came back, the man still dragging the boy and the boy now looking as if he had been

83

beaten almost senseless. Then I did feel sorry for him. He was stumbling blindly along at his father's heels hardly able to lift his feet. Not far from where I sat he suddenly went limp. Feeling him falter, his father lifted him off his feet; otherwise he would surely have pitched to the pavement. As he dangled there by one wrist there passed over his face an expression of dismay followed instantly by no expression whatever, a pallor that almost obliterated his features, weak at best, and then he vomited copiously and at length.

"That boy," I observed to myself, "has been eating too many hot tamales."

He was still retching when his father gave him a shake, set him on his unsteady legs, and viciously kicked him.

"Get to the car!" I heard the man hiss. "Don't even look behind you."

Then my attention was diverted from them. They were going in the opposite direction from the one that other people were going, at a run, all over the square.

On the edge of the crowd, which was impenetrable, I listened to a man tell how Jewel Purdom had first ordered Finus to say how many tamales there were in the package he held out to him, and how Finus, after blinking at him a time or two, had turned his head and looked down at the little boy, staring at him with wonder and consternation. For there had scarcely been time for him to have swallowed, much less chewed, as many hot tamales as were missing now from the baker's dozen he had been given. Finus frowned and shook his head at the boy in remonstrance, perhaps intending also to convey a warning that he was in for an upset stomach, but he failed to effect any change in the increasingly self-preoccupied vacancy of Gilbert's expression.

All of which was taking too long to answer than suited

Jewel Purdom in his present mood. "Didn't you hear me?" he asked. "I said, how many hot tamales is this?"

"I heard you," said Finus, not looking at him. "It's eight."

"Then you *can* count," said Jewel Purdom, his voice rising with his rising anger. "You just figured that little boy couldn't. Or is eight as high as you can go?"

Still Finus did not look up but stared on at the little boy, until at last Gilbert, by then feeling very unwell, said to the author of his discomfort, "Old nigger, you."

Into Finus's face came a look of wild terror. He cried, not to the man menacing him, but to the crowd at large, "Still two for a nickel! Still just two bits a dozen!" No one came to his aid. Falling back against the wall, he began frantically to tear open his shirt, as if his breathing were obstructed, popping off the buttons in his haste. There never was agreement afterwards on what made Finus do that. Some said he wished to show that he was unarmed, the Negro notion of a weapon being a straight razor worn beneath the shirt on a string around the neck. To others he seemed to be baring his chest in defiance, daring the man to do his worst. Still others saw in it a gesture of despair and resignation to his fate.

In any case the unexpectedness of it stayed Jewel Purdom's advance. At this somebody from the crowd intervened, although the man telling about it was prevented by a cough from identifying the person, somebody who knew Jewel and drew him aside, talking to him all the while, and who might have succeeded in cooling him off and getting him away and nothing more have come of the affair if only Finus had kept his big mouth shut. Instead he had chosen the moment to release his cry, "Molly ot! Hot tamales!" louder even than his usual, and sounding, whether he meant it to or not, taunting, derisive, exultant. It may be that in the pasty face of seven-year-old Gilbert

85

Purdom Finus thought he had recognized at last the doom that had stalked him down the years, and now was giving vent to his fear and his relief. He may just have been trying to clear the atmosphere, break the tension, restore things to normal and get back to his business of selling hot tamales. Whatever his intentions, his cry had not ceased reverberating when Jewel Purdom sprang, knife in hand.

As I turned away I heard the speaker say, "No, Otis, I didn't. Not a thing, although I was standing not ten feet away right through it all. I was engaged in conversation with a friend of mine and looking the other way. Never knew anything had happened till people came running up. That's all right. Just sorry I can't be of any help to you."

Otis was Otis Langford, the town constable.

Without their fathers to set them on their shoulders small boys like I was then got to see sights only after their elders had looked their fill. By the time I got near enough to see it the wide pool of blood on the pavement where Finus had fallen was, though still wet, beginning to congeal. An iridescence playing over its surface in waves and slow swirls made it appear to shrink from exposure to the air like a living, that is a dying, thing. The way a fish fresh out of water grows more vivid and lustrous as it struggles and gasps, then fades as it dies, so Finus's blood brightened and shone as I watched, then darkened and lay still beneath a spreading dull film. Just before that final stage, however, came another. Struck by the glare of the sun, the pool of blood became a mirror, and in it I saw reflected—and can see still, though this was long ago and Blossom Prairie now far away—the buildings of the square in sharp perspective, the courthouse tower, the Confederate soldier mounted high on his marble shaft, the steeple of the Methodist church that sat a block away on a hill overlooking the creek.

86

VI

OUR HOUSE all day Sunday was as still as a house in mourning. Worried looks passing between my parents hung heavily over my head. Whenever I glanced up they put away their thoughts, but I could see them still, as I could see the tops showing of bottles put on shelves out of my reach.

That afternoon when I was supposed to be napping I heard my mother say to my father, "What do you reckon they will do to the man that did it?"

My father's newspaper rustled. "You are referring, I suppose," said he, "to yesterday's ruckus on the square, and to the man who—?"

"Well, what on earth else would I be talking about?" my mother cried. Then remembering me, "Ssh!"

"There are other things on earth you might be talking about," returned my father testily, "and I wish you would. However, to answer your question. What will they do to Jewel Purdom, of that ilk, for knifing on dire provocation a lone, unsurvived darky with a reputation for independence and a voice such that even a white man would have to be careful what he said with it? Well, there were, let's say, three dozen witnesses to the event. If the matter ever comes to a trial one dozen of these will testify that they happened to be looking the other way at the time and never saw a thing until it was all over. Another dozen will produce friends and relations to prove they were somewhere else twenty miles away all day long. And the remaining two dozen—"

"You only had three dozen to start with."

"That's right. And the remaining two dozen will swear on their Bible oath that the defendant acted in self-defense. Afterwards in Market Square as the jug is passed around

87

the acquitted and the members of the jury— Why do you ask me foolish questions? You've lived here all your life the same as I have."

"But there were some there who can't be got to say that. Who saw what happened. Yes, I have lived here all my life, and I know there must have been some there who would come forward and—"

"Would you?"

"Me? Why, I wasn't . . ."

"Well?"

"Well yourself! Would you?"

"No, I wouldn't, if it makes you feel any better."

"It doesn't make me feel any better."

"Me neither."

Later that evening my father came in and sat down on the edge of my bed. Before he could speak I said, "Daddy, I don't want to live here any more. Let's move away. Let's go somewhere far—"

My father scowled. "Are you still at it?" he snapped. Hearing himself made his voice turn shrill. "Isn't that about enough of this now? How much longer are you going to mope over that damned nigger?"

I started back, drawing my bedcovers up, and stared at my father aghast, frightened at the violence of his outburst. Under my gaze my father reddened. In his eyes I saw a troubled plea for my forgiveness. My father was not angry at me but at the world which was all he could give me and which he was as helpless to cope with as I.

Monday came.

By afternoon my mother had given up trying to occupy or divert me. I sat at the window watching the empty street. The time drew near when down from above had always sounded Finus's cry. In heavy silence the clock on the mantel tolled four. I felt my chin pucker and tremble, my bruised heart swell with pain. My mother cleared her throat to speak but checked herself, fetching a deep breath instead. Then releasing her breath she said, "Oh, honey, don't try any more to hold it all in. Come to Mama and let yourself go and cry."

For a second I felt myself waver. But I knew the moment was a crucial one for me. It would be a long time before this hour of a weekday afternoon could come without my hearing, wherever I might find myself, the friendly thunder of Finus's voice rolling down from the top of our street; but the time would come. For a while afterwards I would see in the gutter at the curbstone or blown into a corner against a storefront a cornshuck as colorless as if it had been boiled, chewed, sucked dry; but after a time I would not see them any more. It would take many Saturdays before I could pass that spot on the square where Finus's blood had lain on the sidewalk; but I could not live in my town without passing that spot, so that time too would come.

"What!" I cried, tears for Finus, for myself, for my father, for all the world gushing from my eyes, "me cry over an old nigger?"

"Ssh!" said my mother, drawing me to her own heaving breast. "You mustn't say that, hon. Nice people don't use that word."

A Home
Away
from Home

"THINK of it!" said Elgin Floyd to Sybil, his wife. "Just think of it! If they should strike oil we could be millionaires."

"Mmm," said Sybil.

"Millionaires!"

"Mmm. Yes, well, don't go spending it all for a while," said Sybil. "They haven't struck any yet."

"No, but they struck it on Alvah Clayton's place, just eight miles from here. If they can strike oil on that damn fool's land, why not on mine?"

"Why not? You're as big a damn fool as him any day of the week, ain't you? Now what I want to know is this: how far down do they go without hitting anything before they decide to give up?"

"How's that again?"

"I say, how long do they go on boring before they either strike oil or quit?"

"Oh. Why, it all depends. Where they've got good reason

to believe there is oil, why, they'll drill down as much as a mile. Maybe even further."

"How long does that take them? A mile, I mean."

"Depends on what they run into. Where there's lots of rock, for instance, that slows things down."

"In that case I expect they'll be a good while on this one of ours."

"Now on that well of Alvah's—*Mister* Clayton, I mean to say—they were drilling all spring long. Went down fifty-seven hundred feet. Good thing for the Claytons they did strike oil, too; for Alvah never done a lick of work all spring, out there hanging around that derrick from morn till night and getting in the men's way when he ought to been plowing and plant—"

"How big a crew do you suppose they aim to send out here to drill this one of ours?"

"Eh? Crew? Why, on that one of Alvah's they had about a dozen men, sometimes more. Why?"

"And how do you suppose they aim to feed and house all that many men for maybe as long as three or four months?"

"Don't ask me. That's their problem."

"It's a problem, all right, out here in the middle of nowhere. And I think I may have the answer to it. Now where do you suppose a person might round up a dozen bedsteads and springs and mattresses in a hurry, hmm?"

"Why, what would a person want with a doz—?"

"Now then, Elgin, up! I want you to stop daydreaming about being J. P. Rockefeller for a minute and get out of that easy chair and go down to the garden with a spading fork. I want to see a dozen rows of fresh ground turned by nightfall, hear? Where's Geraldine? Geraldine!"

"Yes'm? Directly."

"No, you come here right this minute. Now, Geraldine, how many times do I have to tell you not to go around barefoot? You're going to have feet on you like a pair of flat-irons, if it's not too late already. Slip on some shoes now, you're coming with me. I'll let you out at the store, you can walk back. Elgin, give Geraldine a dollar bill. Geraldine, I want you to buy a flat of tomato plants, four packages of string-bean seeds, two of—"

"Mama, what in the world do you want with all that many seeds and plants? We've already got more stuff growing in that garden than we can put up, much less eat."

"I'm not intending to put them up. I'm expecting company."

"You are! Oh, goodie! Who, if I may ask?"

"Just do as you're told and you'll see. Elgin, give me the key to the truck. I've got lots of running around to do. That tourist camp that just went broke out east of town: there's where I bet you can pick up some beds and things at a bargain."

"Now just a minute," said Elgin. "Just whoa right where you're at, Mrs. Floyd. I see now what you're up to. Well, you can just stop before you go a step further. No, sir, I ain't taking in no boarders."

"Oh, Papa, hush," said Geraldine.

"Take in boarders? People like us, that may be millionaires any day now? No, sir. Not if I know anything about it. You hear me, Sybil? Here's where I set my foot down."

"Careful you don't set it where it's liable to get stepped on, hon. Now when you get back from the store, Geraldine, take and start in on them attic rooms with the broom and the dust mop. When you get done up there—"

"What!" Elgin snorted. "You think anybody will pay to sleep up there in that dusty, hot old attic?"

"No. I think they'll pay to sleep in our rooms while we sleep in that dusty, hot old attic."

.   .   .

93

With half the family's savings Sybil Floyd bought, in addition to the beds and bedclothes, a second cow to add to the one she already milked, a secondhand cream separator, a bigger churn. To her flock of layers she added another four dozen. She bought pullets to raise for fryers. She laid in stores of staple goods. When Elgin saw all the things she had bought he cried, "You talk about me spending money before we've seen it!"

But the geologists and engineers, suntanned men in whipcord riding breeches, lace boots, and suede-leather jackets, who came out in a big dusty misused expensive passenger car to survey the Floyd place, had sampled Sybil's cooking and their praises gave her confidence in herself. "When they strike oil, Elgin, honey," said she, "I want you to spend the money just as fast as you can lay your hands on it. All this is just in case they don't. Now on your feet! I've got another job for you. Get your hammer and saw and follow me. You'll need your pick and shovel, too. A one-holer ain't going to do when there are fifteen of us staying in this house."

Roughnecks, they were called—they gloried in the name. And they looked the part: hard-working, hard-living, coarse, rowdy men. Seeing Geraldine in their midst—a dozen men who had knocked about the world, many of them unmarried, others used to living apart from their wives—Sybil wondered what she had done. Suddenly Sybil's little girl was a big girl. She grew three inches overnight, rounded out as though she had just freshened with milk. The added height was owing to the high-heeled shoes which she would not change for more comfortable ones even when waiting on table. As yet the crewmen were too interested in their food to notice the girl whom their com-

ing had made a woman of. Observing this, Sybil hoped to
keep them well behaved by keeping them well fed.

Fine specimens of men they were—muscular, real men
—big men for a big job of work. Dirty! They would come
clomping in to dinner at noon looking as if they had struck
oil already, only a circle of white around their eyes, black
with grime, machine oil, axle grease. To wash themselves
up before supper they required a hundred gallons of water
boiled in drums in the back yard, blackened two dozen
towels daily. And how they did eat! Geraldine was kept
going at a steady run from the kitchen to the table and
back. Platters of fried steaks, pans of biscuits, stacks of
hoecakes vanished in a trice. For Sybil, even without other
reason, it was hard to remember to be cautious as she
heaped up those platters of food. Keeping a boarding
house was new to her; in her older and more congenial
role as housewife and occasional hostess it flattered her
vanity to see men relish her cooking so.

Her boarders spoke of the countless boardinghouses
which in the course of their footloose lives they had known,
heaping scorn upon the grasping and cheating tribe of professional boardinghouse keepers. Not only to Sybil's face
but among themselves at table they declared loudly that
none could compare with her. Hearing this out in the
kitchen, Sybil felt ashamed of her impulse to stint them,
and taking from the pantry the cutlets or the chops intended for tomorrow's supper, and rousing the fire with a
shake of the ash hopper, she refilled the four big skillets
just beginning to cease to sputter on the range.

For the drilling crew the day's work began at seven,
for Sybil at five. First she split kindling, brought in stove-
wood, and started the fire. Then she milked the cows, separated the cream and churned butter, collected the eggs.
She kneaded dough and stamped out biscuits and when

95

the range was roaring and hopping on its feet and the heat in the kitchen enough to singe your brows, she made breakfast. For each man four fried eggs. Bacon and sausage and fried ham, grits and red gravy, fried potatoes, coffee by the gallon. Breakfast finished, the table cleared, the dishes washed and dried and the table reset, it was time to begin making dinner. There were peas by the bushel to shell and potatoes by the bushel to peel, roasting ears to shuck in stacks like cordwood. There were chickens to kill and pluck and draw, fish to scale, meat to grind. After dinner a dash in the truck into town to shop for the next day while at home Geraldine made the beds and swept, then back in time to scrub and wring and hang out the bedsheets and the towels and iron and start the pies and cakes baking for supper and slice the peaches or the strawberries for ice cream and set Elgin to cranking the freezer. By bedtime Sybil's face was bright red from standing over the range and peering into the oven door, the skin drawn taut, her eyes glazed; and lying beneath the eaves in the attic where the heat made the kitchen seem cool, she passed out murmuring her assent to Elgin's latest plan for where they would go and what they would buy when the money started pouring in.

Elgin could do nothing for hanging around the works all day. All that activity was just too engrossing for a man to tear himself away. To go alone down to the field while all that was going on, to follow behind the mule breaking the stubborn soil beneath a broiling sun while visions of ease filled his mind—Sybil hadn't the heart to nag him. To the tapping of the carpenters' hammers the derrick rose skywards in diminishing X's. The heavy gear was brought in, unloaded from the great tractor trailers, and maneuvered into place. The generator hummed to life, the drilling rig clattered and clanked, the earth shuddered. At night there was a report of their progress: a hundred feet, five hundred feet, a thousand. A thousand feet! As far as out to the chicken house and back down through that stiff red earth which to have to open one foot of with a plow strained a man's back. Elgin's vocabulary blossomed. He spoke of faults, of lignite, of casings, and when they began to break, of diamond-head drilling bits.

Encouraged by their loud and constant praise, Sybil regaled her boarders with more and more tasty and elaborate dishes. The competent-looking and noisy bustle going on outside, the table talk, rich in the jargon of oil, which reached her out in the kitchen, Elgin's enthusiasm, all combined to lull her prudence asleep. The profit she might expect to make from her enterprise came to seem trifling when compared with the fortune she soon might have. To wish to profit from those who were working so hard on her behalf seemed mean. Sybil ceased to consider the crew as paying boarders and began to consider them her guests. Before long in her off moments she was darning their socks, patching their pants, mending and sewing buttons on their shirts: making for the boys a home away from home. To save, she scrimped the family. She and Elgin and Geraldine ate in the kitchen after the men had finished and were sitting around the parlor listening to the battery-set radio which Sybil had provided for their evening entertainment.

By the end of the first month they were down to fifteen hundred feet and the string, as they called it, was drawn out for a test sample. This indicated the kind of soil associated with oil. Elgin was elated and Sybil also was cheered. She had been sobered to learn when the bills from the butcher and the grocer came in that her expenses exceeded her income and that to make up the difference she would have to make a further withdrawal from the family savings account.

They were down to twenty-one hundred feet when one

97

evening just as the men were starting in on second helpings at the table the world exploded and caught fire. The noise was as though the earth were a balloon and a pin had been stuck in it. On the site of the derrick a column of fire too bright to be looked at shot from the ground up to heaven.

"We've struck gas!" groaned the foreman.

"We've struck," said Elgin in tones of awe, "Hell."

A telegram was sent off to the company's head office. Next day a black motorcycle, its noise silenced by the roar of the fire, stopped at the gate in a puff of dust and the driver dismounted.

He looked like a man-sized bug, shiny black, with big yellow bug's eyes sticking out beyond the sides of his head. He wore an aviator's black leather helmet strapped underneath the chin, the immense wraparound goggles, seated on sponge-rubber padding, made of amber glass, reflecting the light like the multicellular eyes of a fly seen under a microscope. He wore a black leather bow tie and a leather jacket with, counting those on the elbows, a dozen zipper pockets, fringed leather gauntlets, black pants as tight as a coat of lacquer, and knee-high black puttees with chrome buckles. Dividing his thorax from his abdomen was a waist no bigger around than a dirtdauber's enclosed in a black kidney belt studded with cat's-eyes in hearts, diamonds, clubs, and spades.

He removed the helmet, disclosing a head as hairless as a hard-boiled egg and of the same whiteness. He had neither eyebrows nor lashes nor trace of beard: all had been burnt away. His features were fixed, rigid, expressionless; only the eyes, beneath their lashless lids, moved. A weathered china doll decorating the grave of a long-dead child was what he reminded Geraldine of.

Judging from appearances he was ageless, but according to the crewmen he was no more than twenty-five. And it would surprise them all if he ever lived to see thirty. In

98

that boy's trade few grew old. If he didn't kill himself on that motorcycle first he would either be burnt up or blown up one day.

What on earth would anybody do it for then? Sybil asked.

Some for the money, others because they were too dumb to know any better, Speed here because he was drawn to flame like a moth and because he loved explosives. For what he was about to do, which in actual work time would amount to maybe half a day, he would be paid two hundred dollars at the least. He, however, though at twenty-five his burns had left him hardly any original skin of his own for further grafts, and though he had one elbow stiffened in a permanent half-bend, was missing a finger on one hand and the thumb on the other, and wore a silver plate in his skull the size of a tea saucer—he would probably have done it without pay. He was an artist—and every bit as temperamental; not with a brush nor with mallet and chisel: an artist in dynamite.

"Well, I just hope he don't blow hisself up here," said Sybil.

"I hope not too," said Geraldine.

"I'd sooner not have the oil than for anything like that to happen," said Sybil.

"Poor little old burnt bashed-up thing!" said Geraldine.

He refused Sybil's offer to fix him a bite to eat. Unfortunately she did not have in the house any RC Cola and Tom's Toasted Peanuts, which according to the crewmen was what he lived on. If she had known he was coming she would have gotten some.

In his firefighting suit, a padded and quilted asbestos coverall as white as his road costume was black, as bulky as the other was sleek, Speed looked more than ever like a bug, this time one wrapped in its cocoon. Again great goggles, these of brown isinglass like the windowpane of a stove, covered his eyes. In this outfit, it soaked with water, he was going to approach the fire carrying a charge of dynamite fused to go off within seconds and drop it down the hole. When told this, and that it was the only way to put out the fire, Sybil said, "Then let it burn." Elgin seconded her. He had decided, he said, that he didn't care any more whether he struck oil.

"You may not," the foreman said, "but we got money down that hole."

From the parlor window Sybil and Geraldine watched up to the point where, carrying his bundle of sticks of dynamite with its sputtering short fuse, Speed got near enough to the blaze to be forced to crawl on his hands and knees. One, two, mother and daughter both passed out. When they came to the fire was out. The gas capped, the crewmen were piping it to the adjacent field. From the escape pipe, ten feet high, it issued with the hiss of five hundred blowtorches. Such was its force that when it was ignited the base of the flame was twenty feet above the opening of the pipe. The flame itself stood six stories tall, pointed and shaped like a blade. The even pressure kept it ever the same. Not even the wind off those Oklahoma plains could sway it.

"How long you reckon it will take to burn itself out?" asked Elgin.

"Got em down south Texas been going like that forty years," said the foreman.

Speed reappeared in his road costume. The women went out to bid him goodbye, Sybil offering up to the time he stomped the starter pedal to fix him a bite to eat, a sandwich for the road, he again with that look of slight nausea in his eyes which the mention of food brought on. He disappeared behind his goggles. He stomped the starter pedal and the cycle roared to life. He lifted his gauntleted hand in a brief farewell.

"Wait! I'm coming with you!" Geraldine yelled. "Can I?"

His reply exceeded in length everything else he had said since his arrival put together. "Hold on you can. Ast for no sidecar. One em thangs on go no fastern a kiddycar."

"Geraldine!" Sybil shrieked. "Get down off of that thing this minute!"

"Mama, you'll have to just manage the best you can without me," said Geraldine, straddling the saddle seat, her skirt three quarters of the way up her thighs, her arms hugging that narrow waist encased in its jeweled kidney belt. "Goodbye. Tell Papa goodbye. I'll write when I get a chance."

Speed twisted the handlebar grip. The engine responded impatiently.

"I hope," Geraldine shouted back, "yawl hit oil."

But although a new derrick was erected and a new string brought in and sent down fifty-one hundred feet, six weeks later the foreman was saying, "Well, Floyd, that's how the dice roll. Sometimes you strike it lucky, sometimes you don't. Right?"

"Yeah," said Elgin. "Yeah, that's right. Sometimes you strike it lucky, sometimes—"

"It's all in the game," said the foreman. "Right?"

"Yeah," said Elgin. "Yeah, that's—"

"Can't bring them all in," said the foreman. "Right?"

"No," said Elgin. "No, you can't bring them all in."

They were dismantling the derrick from the top, throwing down the pieces and stacking them in a trailer. Others meanwhile took apart the toolshed. When they were finished all that was left was the enlarged outhouse which looked now like a boxcar forgotten on a railroad siding, a hole in the ground seven eighths of a mile deep, and an eternal flame. When all the equipment was stowed they drove away. In one truck rode the crew, waving back as they went, beginning already on the box lunches Sybil had packed for them. The Floyds waved until they were out of sight, sighed, and turned back towards the house. Over everything a stillness settled, made more intense by the hiss of the flare.

With only the two of them to cook and keep house for Sybil did not know what to do with herself. She sat in the kitchen or out in the yard peeling potatoes or shelling peas in piddling amounts, rousing herself with a jerk now and again from out of a study, dashing a tear from her eyes from time to time at the memory of Geraldine. Elgin poked about the spot where the derrick had stood, kicking clods. It was too late in the year to think of planting a crop, though how they were to get by without one was hard to figure, Sybil having told him that rather than making a profit on her boardinghouse venture she had used up their savings and owed the butcher and the grocer the bills for the last three weeks. They tried to occupy themselves but they both just moped. Their lives had gone flat. The gas flare made it impossible to do anything. Its light kept them awake, its noise deafened them, its heat scorched them. Too bright to be looked at even in the glare of noon, it illuminated the midnight: a flaming sword, like the one set to guard the east gate of Eden.

"Well, Elgin, never mind, hon," said Sybil. "We've still got our health and we've still got each other. So don't go breaking your heart over that million dollars."

"Aw, for pity's sake, Sybil," said Elgin, "what kind of a fool do you take me for? Do you think I ever really believed we were going to strike oil? Me?"

The
Rainmaker

I

THE HUNDRED-MILE stretch of the Red River from the
Arkansas-Oklahoma line west to Hugo (or if you were on
the other side, from Texarkana west to Paris, Texas) was,
in 1936, served by a single ferry: the one on the Clarksville-
Idabel road. You were, in either case, always on the other
side from the side the ferryboat was on when you drew
up at the landing; and as it had no schedule, not even one
to fall behind in, you could sit there honking till the cows
came home, the ferryboat would cross over for you whenever its owner felt like it and not before. Maybe not then.
For if, in running his trotline as he came across (he hauled
in sometimes as much as twenty pounds of channel cat-
fish), the ferryman should sight an alligator gar, he would
drop his tiller and cut loose with his .30-30—the bullets
whining off the water and over the heads of any waiting
passengers—and he might on such rudderless occasions
fetch up a mile or more downstream from the landing; for
the current is deep-running and strong, though on the surface it does not look as if there is any current; indeed, it

does not look like a liquid, but rather like a bed of red clay, of the consistency of what potters call "slip," and looks as if it would not only be unsuited to any of the uses to which water is generally put, but that getting it to pour would be like starting a new bottle of ketchup.

The ferryboat (raft, really) took but one car at a time. If there should happen to be more than one they just had to wait while the boat went across and came back—an inconvenience which the driver of the lead machine in the field of fourteen bearing down upon the Oklahoma landing one July day in 1936 was counting heavily upon. He was a stranger to those parts, but no stranger to back-road ferries. Neither, however, was he a stranger to the tricks of fate; and should the boat happen to be on the other side, well, he thought, with a glance of his strained and bleary eyes into the rearview mirror, he might as well just as well drive right into the river. And with a glance at the speedometer and a thought for his brake-drum linings, or lack thereof, he might not be able to keep from it if he tried.

By chance the ferry was on the Oklahoma side that day, having been trapped there the previous noon when the wind began to rise and the sky to blacken over. Now the wind had died but the darkness lingered. It was not evening or even very late afternoon, but over everything lay, lower than any cloud, denser than fog or smoke, and of a color like snuff, and almost as acrid, a uniform suspension of fine red dust, so that the air was to air what the river water was to water. And so the ferryman could hear the cars coming long before he could see them, could hear the horns honking steadily as a flight of southering geese and growing louder, nearer, in numbers such as had never before demanded his services at any one time, hardly in any two weeks' period, sounding like a wedding cortege or like a high school celebrating a victory of its football team. So he was ready and waiting for them, with his engine started and idling, the gate chain lowered, his two running lights lit, the hawser poised to cast off and his other hand out for his half dollar. He coughed and spat, thinly and of the color of tobacco juice, though at the moment he was not chewing. This dust was not something raised by the approaching cars; it was the prevailing atmosphere in Oklahoma that spring and summer, and the one before, and the one before that, when with dust storms following one another often not two days apart, dark as night piled on night, it had come to seem almost the native air. This had been one of the worst.

Then the ferryman saw them, the headlights filtering bloodshot and diffuse through the red pall, then saw the line of cars, with one, a truck or a van or a bus, away out in front, the ones in the rear all closely strung together and undulating in waves over the rutty road like the segments of a caterpillar, the horns whooping now like a pack of hounds, and all of them coming at considerable speed— considering, that is, the visibility, the state of the road, and the fact that the combined age of the fourteen cars and pickups running the race was in the neighborhood of two hundred and fifty years.

The river level during the past three rainless years had dropped steadily; now there was a long sandy incline down to the ferry landing. When it reached the top of this bank the winning car was a good hundred yards in the lead. If the driver even paused to see whether the boat was there, it was not apparent to the ferryman. The car came down the bank lurching and swaying from side to side, rattling, the radiator boiling, out of control or with a flat tire or, as was entirely possible from the look of it, with no brakes, picking up momentum as it came and headed for the boat as if with deliberate intent to sink it. The ferryman had no time to shout and barely time to jump. He jumped onto the boat rather than aside on the bank; had he not he would surely have been left ashore, for with the propulsion imparted by the car the boat shot twenty feet out into the water at one bound. It slapped down, scattering spray, bounced again and then again, skipping like a flat skimming stone, the front end leaping so high that whereas in the first moments it had seemed certain the car would plunge over the wheel chocks and through the forward chain, it seemed certain the next moment to roll into the river off the stern. Each time the bow slapped down it lunged forward, then as the bow rose it scurried backwards, and now with the deck awash it began skidding sideways. All this while the ferryman was down on his knees looking as if a mule had kicked him and slipped the knot in that hawser in his hand. The truck heaved a final burp from the radiator, sputtered and died. The ferryman staggered to his feet, fetched breath, and commenced cursing. Clenching his fists, he started forward. From behind him on the shore came a chorus of derisive honks and laughter and shouts.

"You sorry, low-down, no-good, smart-alecking, son of a—" he said.

By then he was alongside the cab. And what so suddenly silenced him was not the bandit's mask, a spotted red bandana, covering from the eyes down the face of his passenger; that was a sight to which the ferryman had grown so accustomed that he hardly noticed it any more during this and the last two dusty summers, when often the entire population of both sides of the river would appear, when issue out of doors at last they must, gotten up as desperadoes, male and female, large and small; and only by oversight—for this had been a bandana day if ever there was one—was he not wearing one himself. No, what stopped the ferryman's tongue while opening still wider his mouth was, that between the two fingers sticking out of the window of the cab was something that looked like a ten-dollar bill, and unless his ears deceived him the voice from behind the bandana had just said to keep the change. At that price he was welcome to take another shot at sinking the boat! Meanwhile there came no shooting from the shore, no *Halt! in the name of the law.* Evidently his passenger was not a fugitive.

What he was, what the whole gang was, the ferryman concluded after a quick appraisal of the vehicle, coupled with the continuing whoops and catcalls from the shore, was a road show of some kind, a small-time carnival, a tent show or a medicine show. The truck—truck or van, bus, whatever the hell it was—was really a house on wheels, with a curtained window in the body just above the cab, and sticking out of the roof a stovepipe out of kilter, and hanging off the rear a rickety flight of steps leading to a door. Along the side was painted a picture (the other side, he would find as he passed it later coming forward to dock in Texas, was, or was as nearly as an amateur hand could make it, a duplicate) in colors whose kindergarten brightness not even the thick coat of dust nor the prevailing duskiness could dim. Hard to say just what the moment intended to be depicted was—the coming of a storm or the passing of one. The sun, of a fiery orange and spoked with beams, was either just emerging from or just going behind a huge inky cloud rent by a jagged bolt of lightning the shape of a flight of stairs in profile, sharpened at the point, rendered in aluminum. Out of the cloud a shower of raindrops was falling, a direct hit from any one of which was apt to prove fatal to the people living in the farmhouse down below or to the two-legged animal (one hind, one front) in the barnlot. Above and below the depicted scene, in a mixture of print and script, small letters and capitals, all staggering and wavy and falling steadily downhill and all bunched together at the end, was a hand-lettered sign.

"Say," said the ferryman, "you fellers a tent show or something?"

"Say," said his passenger, "don't it seem to you like we're kind of drifting?"

The ferryman scooted back to his tiller and nosed back upstream. He shifted gears on his engine. Now he could see the lights from the cars on the Oklahoma shore only dimly, but he could still hear, though unable to make out the words, shouts and laughter. Bunch of cut-ups, he said to himself, who had had a bet among themselves which would get across the river first, not caring a damn how many lives they endangered along the road and obviously not whether they sank his boat and him along with it. Drinking probably. Road-show people. He had ferried their kind across before. Free spenders always. Easy come easy go. He would really rake in the money tonight!

The old engine was in high gear, and presently the ferryman discerned, down at the bottom of his vision, like the sediment at the bottom of a glass of the river water, a darkening, a shoreline: Texas. Then for the first time his passenger poked his head out. He inched it out cautiously as a turtle and looked back towards Oklahoma. There was nothing to be seen, yet in the light of the running lamp on its pole, above the mask the eyes smiled. As Moses must have smiled on reaching the far shore of another body of red water and looking back.

"Say," said the ferryman, stopping on his way forward to dock, "tell me, what does it say here on the side of your truck? I seem to have mislaid my specs." (The letters were a foot high.) He could hardly see the man, not only because it was dark and so little of him was unmasked, but also because of the height of the cab.

"Lost your glasses, eh? Your reading glasses, was they?"

The ferryman said nothing, only gritted his teeth.

"Well, I'll tell you. See that picture? That thundercloud? That bolt of lightning? Them raindrops? What the words spell is, 'Lightning rods for sale.'"

"Can't read a word without my specs," said the ferryman, squinting. "But now that you say so, I can make it out for myself. Lightning rods for sale." Thinking of that ten-dollar bill, and of the weather for the past several years, he said, "Hmm. I wouldn't have thought your business had been so good here lately."

They bumped the dock. The driver started his motor. He revved it. The ferryman threw his hawser and dropped the chain with a clatter. As the driver went past, the ferryman said, "Pull over to the side of the road there if you like and . . ." The rest was finished on a falling cadence—the spoken equivalent of that line of lettering along the side of the truck—as, with a low-gear growl, tail light wigwagging over the bumps, the truck shot up the hill. ". . . and come back with me to . . ." The tail light disappeared. ". . . pickyourbuddiesup."

II

WHEN IT had gone about a mile down the road the truck turned right down a side road running parallel to the river. Over this it jounced and swayed for about a mile until it turned down an even rougher road—"gully" would be a better word—an old logging trail hacked through the tall pines which led back to the river. He was not driving fast now, not only because the road was rough and the dust in the air such that he could not, but because he was safe now. He knew what the ferryman did not know, that he would find no customers waiting for him when he got back to Oklahoma.

He came out of the trees and into a clearing at the river's edge. He drove down as near to the water as he could. Leaving the headlights burning, he got out. Had anybody been there (in which case he would not have gotten out) that person would have seen that the mask and a pair of ankle-top shoes, socks, and supporters was every stitch the man had on. Not that he was exactly nude, but there are no seams in a suit of feathers and tar.

Basically he was white Leghorn, but there was an inter-sprinkling of barred rock, Rhode Island red, some gray goose, some guinea hen, and even some bright bantam rooster, all fluffy and fine, being pinfeathers and eiderdown of the kind and assortment to be expected from the stuffing of a featherbed, saved over the years by some farmwoman from all the poultry killed and plucked for many a Thanksgiving and Christmas and family-reunion dinner. The man's long, red, wrinkled, leathery neck, notched with bones, his crawlike Adam's apple, the wattles underneath his chin and his beak of a nose enforced his resemblance to a chicken—one in molt. His eyes, probably blue, were so bloodshot they were purple. He was bald on the crown, though his straggling reddish-gray hair was long enough to drape over the bare spot ordinarily. But upon his pate someone had recently wiped a paintbrush well charged with creosote and there a solitary pinfeather now stuck up like a cowlick. He was around forty-five years old, a stringy man of medium height who looked taller because of the stoop in his shoulders, the unmistakable stoop of one who from boyhood has followed the plow. He had long stringy arms on the lower parts of which where the feathering was sparse the veins stood out in permanent high relief like the grain in old weathered wood, say the side of an abandoned and never-painted haybarn. He was in a state far past mere weariness, bordering on collapse, and he was swearing steadily, possibly unconsciously, a sort of un-edited imprecation almost as if he were humming to himself without any tune.

He went now around to the back of the van and hauled himself up the steps, opened the door with his shoulder, and fell inside. A crash sounded and a yelp of pain as he stumbled over something. He was out again shortly with a battered pail and a three-foot length of frayed-ended garden hose. He removed the Irish potato that served as a cap to the gas tank, poked the hose down the hole, put the end in his mouth, sucked, spat, and directed the flow into the pail, all with a polish which showed a good deal more practice than could have been gained on a single gas tank. He stepped into the light of the headlamps and, raising the pail shoulder high, poured half the contents over himself. He commenced plucking. In time a pile of sodden feathers lay at his feet; it looked as if half a dozen fryers had been scalded and plucked on the spot. He went back inside the van, returning this time with a thin cake of soap and a napless threadbare towel.

He eased himself into the tepid, opaque water, his head sticking up like a turtle's on that long seamy neck. Taking a deep breath, he ducked under. He came up spitting. He lathered his head and his underarms and his chest and ducked under again and came up spitting once more. He climbed out on the bank and rubbed himself down. When dry, the reddish-gray mat of hair on his chest looked like rusty steel wool. The smell of tar and gasoline had by no means been washed away.

He returned to the van and went inside and lighted a lamp, revealing some kind of broken machine in a heap in the middle of the floor, a huge round one-legged claw-footed dining table, a high-backed hickory-splint rocking chair, an oval dirt-colored rag rug, an immense chifforobe of black wood, three cylinders of cooking gas, a small pot-bellied stove, a woodbox (empty), a two-burner Coleman range on a shelf and on the floor beneath the shelf a coal-oil can with a sodden corncob stopper, an unmade daybed.

A shelf ran high along one wall, and he began searching among the stuff on it. While his back was turned a small tarred and feathered dog, possibly of the rat-terrier breed, divided about equally between dog and long feathered tail, recently very wet and still very moist, slunk up the steps with its tongue lolling and into the room, and trying to make itself still smaller than it was, stole unnoticed underneath the bed.

The assortment of paraphernalia on the shelf included some half-dozen road flares of the kind left by night alongside detour signs, three or four old automobile batteries, two wooden boxes, one opened, the other unopened, labeled EXPLOSIVES, HANDLE WITH CARE, and a collection of apparatus vaguely electrical-looking, including coils and switches and fuse boxes and a hand-cranked generator with a much-worn armature rather resembling a large old-fashioned coffee mill. Behind all this he found what he was looking for (though success in his search brought no pause in that steady mumbled cursing) and began taking them down: quart cans of paint. He pried the lids off. There, scummed over, was the orange of that sun on the side of the van, and there the blackish blue of the cloud and there the red of the barn, the white of the raindrops—when all was dumped together into a pail and stirred, is was the color of mud.

As he stirred, the man regarded two other cans on the shelf above the cookstove. These were cans of tomatoes, with labels like miniatures of the sun painted on the panel of the van. He stopped stirring, rose, and went towards them, his eyes glazed, entranced. Then he caught himself and returned to the paint bucket.

Still naked, he went outside carrying the bucket and a brush, a worn-out broom, and a rickety stepladder. He swept down the side of the truck, coughing at the dust he raised. He stood the ladder beside the truck and climbed it to the top carrying the bucket. The paint was thick; one coat was going to have to do. He started in on top, first turning up the volume of that constant maledictory static he was making, and with three broad strokes of the brush, one of which he had to stretch so far to complete that he almost toppled off the ladder, he slashed through the words:

THe 1 & OnLY ProF. ORViLLe SiMMs

He coughed, stepped down a rung, and painted out the ascending sunrays. Stepping down another rung, he painted out the cloud, the base of the lightning bolt, the face of the sun. He rested a moment, coughing, rubbing his eyes, swearing, then stepped down and painted out the tip of the bolt of lightning, the remainder of the cloud. Then he had to come down off the ladder and rest. He had not slept in thirty-six hours. Not slept? He had not drawn one unterrified breath in all that while! His eyes felt as if all the dust in the world, or at least in Oklahoma, was underneath the lids. He climbed the ladder again and blotted out forevermore the falling raindrops. Stepping down, he painted out the farmhouse and barn and that one sui-generic head of livestock. Then dipping his brush in the paint and not even wiping it on the lip of the pail, with a curse (he would have all this to do again around on the other side), a vicious swipe and a spattering of mud-colored drops, he painted out the large bottom word:

RAiNMAKeR

III

JUST PLAIN unemployed Orville Simms, dressed now in khaki pants and shirt, drove that night until he could drive

113

no farther, until his eyelids began to anneal, his hands to palsy on the wheel, until he began to have waking nightmares of windmill derricks, whole forests of them alongside the road and stretching away into the night, going south now through Red River County and into true night, the vast Texas night, with stars overhead, not the daytime night of dust; and then, after he had awakened barely in time to keep from going off into the ditch for the third time, he pulled off into somebody's cowpasture, started to get out of the cab and go back to his bed, and passed out at the wheel. His sleep was sound—too sound—comatose. He moaned, he whimpered, he twitched. Throughout the night frequent shudders shook him, jerking him almost awake, as in his dreams he felt himself falling from a height. . . .

Two days earlier, in Oklahoma, Prof. Simms was driving down a country road when his radiator came to a boil. The truck was an old enough model to have for a radiator cap one of those round glass gauges with a mercury column inside. It was older than that: not only Prof. Simms but numerous previous owners, though occasions had not been wanting, had come too late ever to see that thermometer rise. What it had long done instead was steam up inside the glass, and in another moment any mercury column would have been invisible anyhow—the whole cap was, the whole front end.

It never occurred to him to look for any standing water in the roadside ditches, where now not even weeds could any longer get a hold, and stockponds that he passed, or what had been stockponds, were dry white scabs covered over with a cracked layer of thin curling crust and invariably with an old car-casing, sometimes an old car, standing half-buried in the middle. Besides, the last three farms he had passed had shown evidence of habitation—

that is, at each one dogs had come out to bark at him as he went past. This boiling of the radiator was a frequent occurrence, and what with that sign along the side of the truck, Prof. Simms had grown timid about stopping to ask for water, even a dipperful to drink. Especially he sought to avoid crossroads stores with their one gas pump and garden watering can meant for radiators, but with also along their porch the usual group of whittlers and spitters. To pull up with that radiator going like a factory whistle at noon and shooting up like Old Faithful when the cap was loosened, and beneath that collective gaze to go and get the watering can was more than the 1 & OnLY ProF. ORViLLe SiMMs, RAiNMAKeR, could take. At such times he especially regretted that self-conferred title of Professor.

Meanwhile the sight of that steaming radiator was a joy to Prof. Simms, and the farther he drove without finding a drop to pour down it, or down his own long dusty gullet, the more joyfully he licked his parched lips with his dry tongue. For fifteen miles he had been driving alongside fields where the cornstalks slanted earthwards and the brown leaves hung tattered and limp and where cotton in scraggly rows stood with bolls which ought long since to have burst white and were instead whole and hard, the shape and the color of and not much bigger than bottled olives. Once he stopped and got out to look closer, and found the earth pimpled and pocked from the last light shower, each pebble perched upon a column of dirt half an inch high and conforming exactly to its outline: a sort of microscopic badlands. Not God's country, perhaps, but the 1 & OnLY ProF. ORViLLe SiMMs's country for sure. If not too far gone even for him.

Just how far gone he learned when he stopped at an abandoned farmhouse for water. He learned then too that the countryside was blessed with the only other thing it needed to make it ideal for his purposes: a long mental drought. He pulled up at the sagging gate and got out and went around back of the house to the well, from the rusty pulley of which hung a bucket that even folks giving up and leaving would not bother to take along. He let it drop, and listened, and heard a sound which, though it augured well for his business, could not but strike an old farmboy as sickening: not the expected sideways slap of an empty bucket striking water, but the dull dry *kachunk* of the bottom of the bucket upon hard dirt. Then behind him he heard a snort of dry, unamused laughter.

"Wasting your time there, Mister," the man said. "Been bone dry since last fall a year. If you're thirsty, step into the house here."

"Thank you just the same. If your well's dry then I don't expect you've got much water to spare."

"Enough to give a thirsty man to drink. When we ain't got that no more then I'll pull out."

"Thank you kindly. But . . . well, I hate to ask it, but what I need is more than just a drink. My radiator's dry. If you're having to haul water, why I'll be glad to buy a bucketful from you."

This suggestion the farmer did not even bother to spurn. Out of the drum he hauled it in he dippered a bucketful of water and, to Prof. Simms's embarrassment, himself toted it out and opened the explosive radiator and poured it in. Poured it in, that is, after letting the radiator cool down, and while waiting he came round and silently studied the picture and text on the side of the truck. After a while he spoke. He did not ask why a man who presumably could call it down from the skies whenever he felt like it had had to stop and beg a bucketful of water from a man who had to haul it in an oil drum from eight miles off, but, apparently unconscious that his illiteracy was a handicap, and certainly not conscious that any stigma attached to it, but rather as if a man who could read and write was something of a curio, if not indeed a freak, asked to know what the words meant. Prof. Simms told him.

"Is that a fact! Well, Mister, I mean Professor, we can sure use you around here! You have sure come to the right place!"

He believed he had. He believed he had. It was almost too good to be true.

"Yes, sir, we been just waiting for you to come along. We been trying to drum us up a rainmaker."

"Is that a fact?"

"Yes, sir. Preachers done all prayed theirselves hoarse. Methodist. Baptist. Campbellite. Adventist. None of them done any good. Last week a gang of us men even went out to the reservation to ask the chief out there if he would have a try. The Indians, you know, they always pray for rain. Not to God, to the Great Spirit. But hellfire, we wasn't particular who sent it, as long as it come. So the men in town they thought it just might do some good and surely do no harm to ask him to see what he could do."

"Yes? What happened?"

"Why, be derned if that old buck didn't turn out to be a deacon in the Presbyterian church! Called us a pack of heathens and run us off his place. As we was piling into the truck to leave another one come up, claimed he was the medicine man and could make it rain pitchforks and nigger babies, but he never looked like he could even make water. The only spirits it looked like he had been in touch with was liquid all right but not water. So it sure looks like you have come to the right place all right, Professor."

"Just when was the last time you folks had rain around here?" Prof. Simms asked.

"Last is right. Last it's ever going to, I was beginning to think. Before you came along, that is."

.   .   .

So he never even had to go to them. All he had to do was drive into town (it was called Arrowhead—he hardly noticed the name, though he was never to forget it) and leave the truck sitting in front of the feed and grain store, and when he came back from the diner picking his teeth half an hour later they were there waiting for him, some two dozen of them.

At first he gave them a flat no. Said he was just passing through their town on his way to another one where his services had been contracted for. He had to agree when one of them said they couldn't need rain over there any worse than they did right here. And furthermore, he said, he never guaranteed a thing. He had his methods, and his methods had been known to work. To work where prayer and witchcraft had failed. Because his were scientific methods. But they ought to know that rain did not come down just whenever you stood up and snapped your fingers. He knew a few more things to do than just snap his fingers. Still, he never guaranteed a thing. He had been known to fail.

Because that was the way to do it: rush right in instead of waiting for some skeptic in the crowd to sneer. This he had learned, as he learned everything, the hard way. At first, when he was just starting out, he had tried to sell himself to the doubters. A big mistake. Once you had done that you had painted yourself into a corner. Then the only way out was to produce. The thing to do was, act as if nobody knew better than you what the odds were against your succeeding. Laugh at them if they even hinted that you set yourself up as infallible. Make them look like fools. Rain? Hardest thing in the world to produce on demand. Yes, that *was* his business. It was a doctor's business to get you well, too, wasn't it? But sometimes you died, didn't you? And when they said they had not had rain in six months, or twelve, and had begun to think it was never going to rain again and didn't see how he or anybody else could hope to make it, say, that's what I think myself. If you folks haven't had rain in all that long a time it looks to me like you ain't never going to get no more, and make as if to leave. Then it was they trying to convince him that he could if he just would, saying, yes, they understood how hard it was, the odds were all against it, they didn't expect the impossible, they would have no kick coming if he failed, only just take their money and do his best for God's sake, try.

But this was the driest, dustiest, thirstiest-looking crew he had ever struck across yet! And the trustingest. They gawked at him as if to say, yes, we understand you don't want to brag. We appreciate it. But you've made your point and shown your manners and so would you please just take our money and say the charm and start the rain, we've been waiting a right long spell. No doubters here. He doubled his usual fee. They swallowed hard all around and looked at one another and licked their lips, and promised to have it for him in the morning—in advance, that is to say, of his performance. A site was fixed upon, one answering to his specification for a windmill or a silo, or some similar elevation. In parting he reminded them again that he didn't promise a thing. As a matter of fact, having consulted *Miles' Almanac* he knew that light showers were forecast for the morrow. He hoped *Miles'* was righter for once than it generally was. He pitied these folks, and his pity was heightened by the thought of what he himself was doing to them. He knew what it was like. He had been a farmer once himself. And he knew what it was to be taken in. His old farm had sat just far enough inside the Arkansas-Oklahoma line to justify the sign that hung on the gap-toothed paling fence, which, once the s's and the e's and the n's and the y's had been unreversed, read:

TRy yOUR LUCk
HUNt fOR OZARk DiMoNds
Big 1s HAVe BeNN FOUNd
1$ peR. HR.

For which in all the years it hung there the only taker he ever got, and this was after he had scratched out the 1$ and made it 50¢, was one wiseacre in a car with a Missouri license tag who stopped one day, and then said on second thoughts he believed he wouldn't after all, because he could tell just by looking that he, Simms, had done already found all the real big ones. Nor had he ever had any much better luck with his other attraction, the cave. Because nobody could stand to set foot inside it and he always had to refund their dime. Even before you stuck your head in, even from fifty feet away, the smell was enough to knock you down. It was the smell of guano, though he learned to call it that only after he had sold out and was packing to leave. The first to call it guano was the man who had bought the place from him, a stranger whom he had taken to be the second diamond prospector, and the first one to think he could tell by looking that he, Simms, had not already found all the big ones, until the man said (this after he, Simms, had tried everything, including drilling another dry hole every time a fresh breeze blew up from Texas with a whiff of petroleum on it, including even farming the damned place), "Diamonds? You trying to be funny? I'm going after that guano. There must be half a million tons of it in there."

"That what?" said Simms.

"Bat shit to you. Most valuable fertilizer in the world. My God, you have got a gold mine in that cave. I mean, I have got a gold mine in it."

And so, feeling sorry for these Arrowhead folks, he

determined to give them a good show for their money. The rainmaker's art, as Prof. Simms had been quick to learn, consisted entirely in this: to make the audience forget what they had come to see, then get away before they recollected. Providentially it worked out that the people most willing to pay for rain were those who were the easiest to beguile, being the ones to whom amusements and spectacles were the greatest rarity.

The production, or as Prof. Simms preferred to style it, in order to stress its experimental nature, "the trial," was set to take place on a farm known as the old Maddox place, chosen because it answered to the Professor's stipulation for a windmill, and because it stood on what passed in those parts for a hill and thus served as a signal beacon and center for community gatherings. From his overnight campsite on the edge of town Prof. Simms set off the next morning bright and early—and a very bright morning it was, with the sky glowing behind the sun like the reflector of a heater—to find the place. He did not have to ask the way. He had only to fall in with the traffic already clogging the road. The line included passenger cars and pickups, motorcycles with sidecars, buggies and wagons, more than one of them its bed loaded with empty barrels, oil drums, washtubs, to catch the rain and carry it back home in. This testimony of simple faith in his powers touched Prof. Simms. Seeing his van, the drivers of the vehicles pulled off into the ditch, the people on foot stood aside to let him pass. Kids sitting along the tailgates of the wagons dangling their rusty bare feet gaped at him as he went by, the women ducked their chins in a quick shy curtsey, the men bared their heads. They were certainly a dry-looking bunch! Their lips chapped and cracked from constant licking, mouths hanging open, their expressions fixed, baked on, they looked like those characters in the moving pictures shown stumbling across Death Valley towards some mirage of an oasis. Near the head of the procession he passed two wagonloads of people dressed all in white nightgowns. In his or her hands each of them clasped a small black book. Even more like wanderers in the desert, their eyes trained on a vision, these folks in their nightgowns looked. Converts, believers in total immersion, they had been a long time waiting for baptism; now beatific smiles wreathed their parched and peeling lips. Prof. Simms was moved, and he renewed his vow to put on a good show for these folks, take their minds off their troubles for one day, at least.

Waiting on the site already were still more. Some looked as if they had spent the night there. Prof. Simms had barely arrived when, passing among the crowd on his inspection of the grounds, he overheard the following exchange:

"When is the rain going to start, Papa?"

"In a minute, son. Give the man time."

"Brung along the family, have you, Dunc?"

"Just this'n here. He ain't never seen rain. Not that he remembers."

Looking down, Prof. Simms saw a boy of four, going on five. He was dressed for the outing in a new yellow oilskin slicker, with a matching sou'wester, and a pair of rubber boots. The slicker having been bought three or four sizes too big, so that he might grow into it, the little boy rattled around inside it like the clapper inside a bell.

By eight o'clock it looked as if everybody had come who was going to come. Gathered on the field were five to six hundred people, young and old, white, black, and red. From the top step of his van Prof. Simms, his fee in his pocket, addressed the crowd in these words:

"Folks, if we're all here I will ask you now to give me

your attention, please, while I explain just what we are going to do."

From the audience arose a silence so profound that he could hear the regular breathlike swish of the palm-leaf fans with which the ladies fanned their faces. Before him were ranged five hundred open mouths, as though awaiting the consecrated host.

"I will tell you everything," he continued. "I mean to keep nothing from you. There is no mystery, no magic, to making rain. It is a science, and science has no secrets. I am not here to mystify you good people with a lot of hocus-pocus. I am not going to lead you all in prayer. I am not going to daub myself with paint and dance around in a ring rattling a gourd. All that is known of the science of rain-making I mean to put to use here today for the benefit of you folks; any man who claims to know more is either fooling you or fooling himself."

Prof. Simms paused to wipe his forehead with his bandana. Lord, it was a scorcher of a day! Imagine anybody simple enough to believe that anybody else could make rain fall from a sky like that!

Rain, the Professor mused; what was rain? Not being scientists, they perhaps thought that rain was water. Well, they were only partly right. There was something else in rain besides water, as anybody could testify who had ever let a bucketful of rainwater settle for a while: dirt. And he proceeded to explain how, according to the findings of science, every drop of rain contained, was formed around, a single grain of dust. So the first thing they were going to do this morning was to raise a little dust.

He turned and disappeared into the recesses of his van. When he came forth again some moments later he was carrying a crate on which in large red letters was stenciled DYNAMITE, and on top of the crate a detonator and several coils of wire.

Prof. Simms directed the digging by volunteers of four holes, one at each corner of the field, and the placing therein of half a stick of dynamite each. Wires were then laid from these to the detonator. Even as he went about this first number on his program, Prof. Simms was mindful to raise an occasional glance to the bright, blank heavens, and to follow this with a slow, slight shake of his head. This show of doubt cost you nothing of your expert standing; it lent you a human touch, meanwhile it opened, by a crack, the door out by which you were going to have to excuse yourself later on.

When the charges had been laid, capped, and fused, the crowd was advised to draw close together and to sit down on the ground. Children were gathered to their mothers. An expectant hush settled over them. Prof. Simms pushed the plunger. Four simultaneous muffled booms went up, raising four geysers of red dust. Gravel rained down upon the people's heads. Pebbles rattled on the hard ground. As the dust cleared Prof. Simms studied the faces of his audience. Usually the dynamite blasts could be counted on to loosen a crowd up, enliven them, begin to distract their minds. This bunch just lifted their dust-powdered heads and gaped at him, waiting to see what was coming next. Among five hundred faces scarcely half a dozen smiles were to be counted. Even the kids were a solemn lot. It was a very single-minded crowd.

Having astonished his audience with the information that rain was something more than water, Prof. Simms next informed them that water was really a gas, in liquid form. Rather, two gases: hydrogen and oxygen. H_2O. To make this go down he employed another homely illustration. When you boiled water on the range, what happened? It went off into the air in the form of a gas, steam. And when you put a lid on the pot it condensed back into a liquid. Now they had the dust that was needed for the drops

to form around up there in the atmosphere; the next thing
was . . .

Again he went inside the van, emerging this time with
three cylinders of cooking gas on a hand truck, two of
them labeled HYDROGEN, the third OXYGEN. He went inside
once more and came back with a carton of rubber balloons.
For the next three quarters of an hour Prof. Simms was
kept busy inflating balloons and tying their necks and
passing them to the kids who had volunteered to hold them.
When all the balloons were blown up he again went inside
his van, returning this time with an automatic .22 rifle. He
called for a volunteer from the audience who was a crack
shot. Nominations closed upon a single name, and after
some coaxing a cross-eyed youth of twenty came forward
dragging one foot and grinning bashfully. Prof. Simms gave
him the rifle and a box of cartridges.

The balloon holders were divided into teams, like con-
testants in an unequal spelling bee, Oxygens on one side,
Hydrogens, two to one, on the other.

"Now then, when I say 'Go!'" said Prof. Simms, "the
first of you Oxygens and the first two of you Hydrogens let
go of your balloons, and you"—turning to the rifleman—
"hold your fire until I tell you, then as quick as you can,
bust all three balloons. Don't miss any or we'll get the
wrong proportions. Go!"

Three balloons, a blue one, a red one, and a yellow one,
soared aloft. The cross-eyed youth raised the rifle to his
shoulder, blinking at the glare, wetting his lips. Up, up,
the balloons soared, smaller and smaller. The rifleman
licked his lips more rapidly. At last:

"Fire!" said the Professor.

Three cracks: three clean hits. The balloons disappeared. Tatters of colored rubber fluttered to earth. *Go!
Fire! Go! Fire!* So for the next half hour. The kids were
diverted, but as for their parents and grandparents, they

turned their faces up, observed the bursts high overhead, then looked down, looked at him to see what was coming next. There was not a smile among them, not even a kindling of interest, just patience, stolid, dumb, unimaginative patience. Not that they were skeptical. On the contrary, with these people a problem different from the one he was used to coping with began to disclose itself to Prof. Simms. Folks generally had to be convinced that he could make it rain; these were going to have to be convinced that he couldn't. Prof. Simms felt a moment's panic. He had put down his toe and found that he was swimming in depths of gullibility over his head.

Prof. Simms next brought out his rockets. The first of these was launched at half past ten. It burst with a satisfying bang, placing a puff of white smoke high above, the only thing visible in the vast, empty sky. He sent up, at a dollar and thirty cents apiece, two dozen of them. As each went off he studied the upturned faces. Ordinarily a fireworks display tickled them so they forgot everything else; when they remembered, and realized that in fact no rain had fallen (by which time he was in the neighboring county), they said, well, he had put on a dern good show, that alone was worth the price. But though fireworks must have been a rarer event in their lives than in most, this crowd could think of just one thing. Dynamite, balloons, rockets: all this excitement they had had, and still they stood there solemn as a convention of cigar-store Indians, waiting for rain. He had, however, one trick left: a performance on Old Magnet. If that didn't get them, nothing would.

Magnet, the *pièce de résistance* of his act, was an invention, rather a collage, of Prof. Simms's own. Ordinarily Old Magnet had merely to make her appearance for somebody in the crowd to declare, " 'Fore God!" or words to that effect, "Would you just look a-here what's coming now! I

George, Sam, if that contraption can't make it rain, be about the only thing it can't do, won't it? Sounds," the speaker was apt to observe, as soon as Prof. Simms began fiddling with the dials, "like she's clearing her throat to get ready to say something." Which in fact she once did. Suddenly remembering her long-dormant, not to say dead, function, she brought in station KRLD, Dallas, and gave out five whole minutes of Chicago cotton and grain futures before she could be tuned out. However, an early-model battery-set radio was merely a part of Old Magnet. Above a bank of switches like the manual of an organ were arrayed needle gauges, fuses, the works from a telephone box, the exposed coil from a Model-T Ford, more vacuum tubes, an electrical rheumatism cure, and a great deal more junk the origin of which Prof. Simms himself did not know. Leading off all this was a long coil of wire attached to a large horseshoe magnet.

For, as Prof. Simms explained—unless there was somebody in the audience to do it for him, and generally there was: some know-it-all who would save him the necessity of a further lecture, and to whom the Professor would listen with a quizzical brow and a half smile, although if there were not, as here, he employed the same explanation himself—it was your magnetism that drew all your other elements together. That charged your dust particles and made them draw your atoms of oxygen and hydrogen and form your drops which your clouds then soaked up. For a cloud was nothing more nor less than a sort of sponge, as you might say, a dry sponge looking for some water. There were your clouds (they still hung there, unmoving, not a breath of wind to stir them, hardly a breath of breath); your dust and your oxygen and your hydrogen were there. Now the thing was, to send up some magnetism. If that didn't do it . . .

Well, if that didn't do it, then the only thing to say was,

there were times and places when all the advancements of
science were to no avail. Time to begin to take the moral
approach, or rather *re*proach. Half jokingly now, to be
borne down on harder a little later on. But as of now to
say, "Well, if what we're about to do next don't turn the
trick, then it's for you folks to say why, not me. I don't
know what you all have been up to, but if the Good Lord is
displeased with you—and that's about the only thing I can
think of to explain a sky like that after all we've done—why
then you realize, of course, that Albert Einstein himself if
he was here couldn't make it rain. It's for you all to say
why He is down on you; but till you folks make it right with
the Lord, why, I'm just wasting my time and talents. When
all's said and done, He's the one that's got His hand on the
hydrant, you know."

To this, as to everything else, they listened without so
much as nodding their heads—never even scratched them.
Even that little boy in the slicker, following at his heels as
he played the wire off the coil to the base of the windmill,
just gaped solemnly at him.

An assistant from the audience was instructed in what
order to throw the switches once Prof. Simms was on top
of the windmill. He stood at the base of it, the horseshoe
tucked into his belt, the wire trailing from him, looking up
at the fan. Prof. Simms disliked heights, and he never
failed at this point to think, surely there must be a better
way than this to make a living. Taking a deep breath, he
commenced hauling himself up the rungs of the tall, narrow ladder.

Just beneath the fan blades a narrow platform ran
around the derrick. Standing on this platform the Professor signaled to his assistant down on the ground. Grasping the derrick with one hand, with the other he pointed
the magnet out into space. Hardly was the last switch

thrown when over the horizon appeared a huge black cloud. "Great God!" gasped Prof. Simms.

Recovering himself at once, he said, "Don't be a fool, like those down on the ground, Orville."

But even as he said this the cloud doubled in size. "If you didn't know better," said Prof. Simms, "blessed if you wouldn't almost believe there was something in it." And despite himself a small shudder of fear, of awe ran through him—fear of, awe of himself.

Meanwhile the people down on the ground had not yet seen his cloud. He leaned as far out from the derrick as he safely could, holding out his magnet. Slowly he drew it back to his chest. Be damned if the cloud didn't leap to follow it! He repeated the gesture: again the cloud raced nearer as if in response. "Well! If this don't beat anything I ever saw!" said Prof. Simms.

Now the people down below saw it. Heads snapped around in that direction and fingers pointed and even up on his perch Prof. Simms heard the universal intake of breath. Three or four times more he repeated his gesture of drawing the cloud on with his magnet, and each time it leaped obediently to follow. The whole sky in that direction, from the ground up to the dome, was now solid black.

A gust of wind whipped his face, followed by another which shook the derrick and turned the fan blades over a couple of revolutions. Prof. Simms looked down. "There! That ought to satisfy you!" he said. He laughed to see them scurrying for shelter down below, drawing their jackets over their heads, whipping up the teams of their wagons, some diving underneath the wagonbeds. He had not long to gloat, however; a blast of wind shivered the derrick, very nearly plucking him off. The fan blades spun. He decided to climb down. He put his foot on the first rung of the ladder, looked down, and saw nothing. People, wagons, his own van, the base of the windmill, everything had disappeared. At that moment he got an eyeful of dust. In anther moment all thought of getting down was put out of his mind by the blast.

And there, like a possum up a persimmon tree, clinging for dear life, while the derrick shook and shuddered and the dust came at him like a sandblast and the fan blades whirred like an airplane propeller, his eyes squeezed shut, the 1 & OnLY ProF. ORViLLe SiMMs spent the next twenty-four hours.

At the end of that time, when the wind had died and over everything had settled a Pompeian silence, Prof. Simms ventured down to reconnoiter. Halfway down he still could not see the ground. At that point he paused to listen. It was then that he noticed for the first time the smell, like a freshly surfaced asphalt road; but hearing no sound, he figured they were all still indoors or in the storm cellar, unaware that the storm had stopped, and that this was the moment to make his break. So he went down farther. Then he saw them. They were squatting around the base of the derrick waiting for him like a party of hunters waiting for a treed coon to come down. Like himself, they wore bandanas over their faces, only to them it lent the sinister look of a band of vigilantes. Halting in his descent, he called down, "Well, I told you all I never guaranteed anything, didn't I?"

No one responded. They didn't even look up. In the silence he heard the familiar whimper of a dog. That smell he had noticed earlier rose more sharply on the still air. Like asphalt, or like a new telephone pole, freshly creosoted. He saw a fire; on it an oil drum steamed. The society below, he now noticed, was exclusively male. He scampered hastily back up the ladder four or five rungs. "Dern it!" he cried. "Whose idea was this anyhow, yawl's or mine?" He clambered back up into the protective gloom and to that rung of the ladder he clung for another hour, calling down from time to time, "Maybe yawl would like a refund? Hey? What do you say to that? Maybe yawl would like a refund, hey?"

IV

WHEN SIMMS woke up in Texas he thought at first that he was still asleep and having nightmares. All around him for as far as the eye could stretch stood windmills thick as trees. He closed his eyes with a shudder, opened them and looked again. They were still there, but now he noticed that they lacked fans. Not windmills, then: oil-well derricks.

After breakfast, at which he was reunited with Samson, his dog, and after plucking Samson of his feathers, Simms drove down the road to the first gas station and general store he came to. Along the porch sat half a dozen men. Simms thought he had seen ignorant, backwoods, gate-mouthed, dull-eyed faces in Oklahoma, and before that in Arkansas, but here . . . Well, he was about ready to restore the sign on his truck. Memories of Arrowhead braked that thought. But before he knew it he had asked, "Been this dry hereabouts for a good spell, has it?"

"Dry? Mister, 'dry' don't cover it. They haven't invented the word yet for the weather we been having."

"Crops all burnt up, are they?" asked Simms, trying to look sympathetic and not grin.

"Ain't much left in the way of crops around here."

"Folks having to haul water, are they?"

"If they are I just wish you'd tell me where they're finding it."

"Ain't nobody much trying to raise crops around here no more. Folks in this section have done all give up farming just about."

"How much rainfall you folks had this year?"

"Oh, Lord, Mister, we done all just about forgot what rain looks like, ain't that right, O.B.? When do you reckon was the last time we seen rain?"

"Well, let's see. I remember it was raining when my wife was fixing to have our last boy. The last boy, that is, not the girl. And only yesterday she had to warsh his mouth out with soap for using dirty talk. He's precocious, still that'll give you some idea."

"What did she use for water?" asked one of the others.

"Wellsir," said a third, "I have paid up to six bits a pint for it right on the streets of Delco. R. D. Blair, that's got that deep artesian well, why my godamighty he's made more money off of that thing than most men has off of oil wells. I've seen bottled water go for twenty-five cents one of them little bitty old Dixie cups full. It's got so around here we dilute our water with whiskey, stranger. Costs too derned much to drink it straight."

"Is it water you're talking about? Selling drinking water on the streets? In bottles? In paper cups? Like soda pop?"

"Naw, sir, not like soda pop. Soda pop don't cost but two bits a bottle. And if you take my advice you'll keep away from it. Won't nothing raise a thirst like a bottle of that damn pop. Worse than salted peanuts."

"Well! I thought I'd seen dry sections of the country before, but this sure beats them all."

"Yes, Lord, I reckon the man that comes up with a way to turn crude oil into drinking water will make him a killing here in Texas."

"I hear they're fixing to bring it out in powdered form soon now."

"Fixing to bring what out in powder form, Gus?"

"Water. Powdered water. Dehydrated. When you're ready to use it you take and mix it with a little water. They say it makes a pretty fair substitute. Tastes a little flat, they say, but does all right for mixing."

"Lord, what won't they they think of next, eh?"

It was true what those men said, people thereabouts had all given up farming; but drought was not their reason. They did not need to farm, not with oil wells pumping away in front and back yards and stretching away over former cotton fields for as far as a man could see. If they needed water it was not for the sake of their crops. They could use some to float those cabin cruisers in the one-time lakes that Simms passed. A bit for an occasional bath, maybe, and to water their flowerbeds. Mainly to wash those big Cadillacs and Packards and Pierce-Arrows that stood, sometimes double-parked, outside their cabin doors. They could pay for it, too, as no dirt farmer worried about his crops and his thirsty livestock could ever afford to pay. So in the hardware store in Delco Simms said to the clerk, "Housepaint. Want some housepaint. Gimme a gallon of the white, quart of red, quart of yellow, quart of blue, and a pint-size can of aluminum. Don't bother to wrap them."

V

THE DAY fixed upon for his performance was just the worst sort of day. With no assistance from Prof. Simms, the sky had clouded over and now thunder commenced to rumble. It was going to rain. You could smell it, could read the signs: birds bunched together along electric wires, leaves of trees showing their undersides, smells sharpening, sounds deepening. After three unbroken years of drought, today it was going to rain, and before he could lay claim to it. He pitched in frantically, trying to get set up and going before it actually started coming down, make it look as if he had a little something to do with it; but even as he tore around, the first drops fell, fat warm drops that struck the hard, unabsorbent earth with a *spat* and scattered in droplets like quicksilver. Prof. Simms only hoped there were others in the audience like the one he overheard say, "Well, if this feller ain't a cutter! He don't even hardly have to do nothing to make it rain, does he?"

The elevation this time was the tower of the county courthouse, seven stories tall. The crowd, biggest he had ever drawn, was gathered on the courthouse grounds. It was to have been the grandest production Prof. Simms had ever staged: a Texas-sized production—was he not being paid a Texas-sized fee? What a stupendous plan he had devised for the dynamite blasts! What a store of skyrockets he had provided! Magnet, inconsiderately tossed inside the van by the mob at Arrowhead, had been refurbished, improved by the addition of a sparkplug tester and something else found on the town dump which Prof. Simms judged to be part of the works of an X-ray machine, and which, when a current was sent through it, reacted with a most impressive crackle. He had been looking forward to the show himself. Was anything on earth as undependable as the weather?

There was no postponing it: no rainchecks on a rainmaking. The timing was set. Ready or not, rain or shine, on the stroke of ten from the courthouse clock things would get underway with a bang. Four bangs, to be exact.

Observing that the signs looked promising, Prof. Simms, face dripping, soaked to the skin, began his address to the crowd. He disavowed magic and mystery. His was a science, he said, and science—here he had to raise his voice to make himself heard above the patter—had no secrets. It was coming down harder every moment as he explained the origin and composition of raindrops, the need to raise some dust. The clock overhead wound itself up to strike. Prof. Simms brought down his upraised hand and the earth shook as sixty sticks of dynamite, fifteen to each of four charges, went off outside the city limits. But instead of the cloud of dust that was to have arisen, down fell a torrent of rain.

Just my luck, thought Prof. Simms, looking down from the top of the courthouse steps upon the umbrellas popping up like mushrooms all over the grounds. Maddening to think that those umbrellas, faded from disuse, dotted with holes, had been brought there out of faith in his powers. His hand stole to his pocket and fondled regretfully the fat roll of bills nestled there. For a moment he toyed with the thought of absconding with it. For only a moment, though; then he remembered the tales he had always heard about Texans, how mean they were, how dangerous it was to trifle with one of them. In tones forlorn he silently chanted, "Rain, rain, go away, come again another day, little Orville wants to play."

"Will wonders never cease!" Prof. Simms exclaimed to himself when the rain promptly complied with his request. The sky brightened by several shades. It was probably as well, however, that precipitation did not cease entirely, just slackened off to a steady drizzle; for Prof. Simms was not there to prevent rain, after all, as to some credulous minds he might appear to have done. Moreover, this was only a lull in the storm; from the west fresh battalions of clouds were moving up, dark as the one in the sign on his van. Could he—perhaps by dropping one act, say the sky-rockets, from his program—be ready for it when it got there? Nothing ventured, nothing gained.

In his race against the advancing storm clouds, Prof. Simms explained the molecular structure of water while at the same time inflating his balloons. For the occasion three instead of the usual one marksman were recruited and armed with rifles. The first release of balloons numbered nine, in proportions proper to the valence of the elements. But before a shot could be fired, even as the word "Fire!" was already in Prof. Simms's mouth, such a cloudburst poured down it was enough to make a person wonder whether God had broken the promise He made to Noah of old.

This was no passing shower, this was the real thing, good for all day and into the night, if Prof. Simms was any judge. "Well, old hoss," he consoled himself, "you did your best. The elements were against you. Better luck next time." Giving the bankroll one last feel, peering through the gaps in the curtain of rain, he searched the crowd for the faces of the men with whom he had contracted for to-day's performance, intending to refund their money. He could not discover them. What Prof. Simms discovered instead was one of those insights that can change the lives of men and alter the shape of history. He saw all those faces looking up at him, streaming wet, waiting patiently to see what he was going to do next, cupping their ears to hear him, hushing up their children whining to be taken in out of the wet, their heads still nodding in conviction, comprehension of his last-spoken words. Modesty, and a life-long inclination to think too well of people, almost made Prof. Simms deny the moment of his greatness. Nobody could be that stup— Through a momentary parting in the curtain, he looked again. You could have heard a pin drop in the silence of Prof. Simms's mind.

"*Orville, my friend,*" he said to himself in an awestruck whisper, "*if you had just half the belief in yourself these folks have in you, you could be governor of this state.*"

By seven o'clock in the evening the county records had been twice removed: first from the flooded basement to the ground floor, thence to the second floor of the courthouse. Since half past four the building had been without electricity, at six telephone service was disrupted. To have stepped outdoors would have been to commit suicide by drowning, therefore those who had taken shelter and were now trapped inside were resigned to going supperless and to spending the night sleeping on the floors, the women and children in the offices, the courtrooms, and the judges' chambers, the men in the corridors.

By that hour Prof. Simms had for some while felt himself to be the target of resentful looks and the subject of discontented mutterings. So when the committee of three men who had contracted with him for his services came seeking him out, he was expecting them. One look at their faces and Prof. Simms thought he detected the odor of warm tar, and he felt himself break out all over in goose feathers.

"Well, Professor!" said the first man, and stood waiting for an answer. He was a burly six-footer whose bone-crushing grip Prof. Simms remembered from the handshake with which they had sealed their agreement.

"Kind of let things get out of hand, ain't you, Professor?" said the second.

"Rain, we said," said the third. "But this—!"

All were silent, Prof. Simms in expectation of violence, they awaiting some practical proposal from him. This was revealed when, none forthcoming, they made their own. Speaking one after the other, the three said:

"So without further ado, maybe you better climb back up the tower—"

"—and put that machine of yours into rearverse gear—"

"—and de-magnetize things, 'fore you drownd us all."

He had learned his lesson, and in commending himself to his Maker, here is what Prof. Simms said:

"Dear Lord, listen to a con man's prayer. Looking to the

future—if I am allowed to have any—please show me the way to some other part of Your creation where You distributed a little bit more sense. Some place where—how does it go?—where you can fool some of the people all of the time and all of the people some of the time, but deliver me, Lord, from a place where you can fool all of the people all of the time. Amen."

VI

THE RIVER, after three days and nights, had returned to its banks and on both sides the roads to the ferry landing were now passable. But anybody who thought he was going to buck that current for fifty cents or for that matter fifty dollars had another think coming to him. They could sit there honking till their arms dropped off.

A ferryman's life was just one blamed thing after another. A week ago you couldn't see to blow your nose for the dust; now this. Not a drop of rain for three blessed years, then all of a sudden floods. It was like God had been out of the office all that while and returned to find all those prayers for rain piled up on His desk. It did seem like He might have used a little better judgment than to answer them all at once.

What a time it had been! Rain rain rain—you couldn't see to blow your nose for the rain. River rising and the banks crumbling in, levees washing out. Cabins coming floating down, some with families sitting on the rooftops, black and white, men, women, children, babies at the breast, old grandfolks. One with a nanny goat astraddle of the peak. Later, town shanties with street numbers on the doors. Trees. Wagonbeds. Chicken coops. Barrels. Cows. Hogs. Mules. And there were people who expected him to ferry them across this! Like the one idiot this morning who came dashing up, said he just had to get over to Texas, and asked how much it would cost. "Two hundred dollars," he had replied. "Then you'll own the boat and can ferry your own self across." Like that one in the truck over there right now—truck or van, bus, whatever the hell it was, with a sign painted on its side—honking as if his life depended on it.

The Pump

FOR WEEKS Jordan Terry had been down on his knees promising God to drink the first barrelful if only they would go on drilling and not give up; but they were about ready to haul out the rig and call it another dry hole, when at fifty-nine hundred feet they brought in a gusher. Jordan was digging turnips in a field that he was being paid by the government not to grow anything on when he got the news, and though he went out and drank a barrelful all right, it wasn't oil.

A day or so later old Jordan was rocking on his front porch and smoking a White Owl when he saw a couple of men of the drilling crew up on top of his derrick with hammers and crowbars taking it apart. Barefoot as he was he jumped out of his rocker and tore down to see what the hell was going on. They told him they were fixing to cap his well.

"Cap it?" cried Jordan with a white face. "Put ere a cap on it? Why? For God's sake, Misters, let her come! Don't go a-putting ere a cap on it!"

They explained that the derrick was just for the drilling. Like a pile driver. There was no further need of it now. They were fixing to install a pump.

"Pump? What do we need ere a pump for?" asked Jordan, remembering how it had shot up in the air, like Old Faithful. "The way it spurted out?"

141

"It's like opening a bottle of beer, ol' hoss," said the chief engineer. "That first little bit that foams over comes by itself. The rest you have to work for."

Work! Hah! Set on your ass in a rocking chair and knock down two bits on every barrelful! That kind of work suited old Jordan to a T.

So the derrick was dismantled and taken away and in its stead the pump was set up. It was like an off-balance seesaw, a beam the size of a crosstie set off-center in the notch of an upright post. To either end of the beam was attached a rod which disappeared into the ground. Up and down it went, up and down, bowing in frenzied, untiring obeisance. Yes, sir, it said to Jordan, you're the boss! Yes, sir, you're the boss! Yes, sir! Listening with your ear to the ground you could hear, or could fancy that you did, a sound like a seashell makes, of endless vast waves lapping the shores of a vast underground sea. And in the pipe you could hear the mighty surge, like the pulse of a great artery drawing up a steady stream of rich, black blood. Day and night the pump went, night and day, working for him: rocket-a-bump, rocket-a-bump, rocket-a-bump . . . In the daytime it went at about the same trot that Jordan went at in his rocking chair, at night as he lay awake grinning in the dark each stroke of the cycle matched a beat of his heart: rocket-a-bump, rocket-a-bump, rocket-a-bump . . .

"How much you reckon she draws every time she goes up and down?" he asked the engineers.

They told him how many barrels it pumped per day. Jordan worked it out from there. He wanted to know just how much he was worth by the minute, how much richer he had grown with each rock of his rocker, each beat of his heart. He got twenty-five cents a barrel. A barrel held fifty-five gallons. It averaged twenty-five strokes a minute. Call it half a cent a stroke. Rocket-a-bump: half a cent. Rocket-a-bump: that makes a penny. Rocket-a-bump, rocket-a-bump—the last thing he heard at night, the first thing he heard in the morning. Sixty times twenty-five was fifteen hundred. Twenty-four times fifteen hundred times three hundred and sixty-five . . .

Jordan—though he was far from being its first owner —had for some years been driving a 1921 Durant. Driving it, that is to say, whenever it felt like going. And only now did he possess somewhere about the amount of oil it demanded. Naturally a man in his position couldn't be seen around in that old flivver any more. As even the hungriest car dealer was not going to allow him anything for it on a trade-in, it occurred to Jordan that he would be doing a mighty fine deed by making a present of it to his next-door neighbor, Clarence Bywaters. Poor son of a bitch. It must be hard on a man to have oil struck right next door to you. Like a canary bird in a cage hung out of a window, and having to watch a fat sassy old blue jay hopping about in the trees and plucking juicy worms out of the ground. They had begun drilling on poor old Clarence's land even before Jordan's, and they were still at it, but only because they had poured so much money down that dry hole that they just hated to call it quits. They were talking about pulling out any day now. Jordan remembered what he had gone through. He didn't think Bywaters would take exception to his offer. Poor son of a bitch, with all that raft of kids he wasn't in any position to despise a little charity.

Delivery on a new Duesenberg, especially one with as many custom accessories as Jordan had put in for, took some time. Meanwhile he still went about in the old Durant. He hadn't gotten around to giving it to Clarence Bywaters when the news broke one morning that they had brought in a gusher on his neighbor's holdings.

Jordan Terry was not the sort to begrudge another his

good fortune. Christ, he had his! He went over and took Clarence Bywaters by the hand and congratulated him. He could not help mentioning his intention to have given him the Durant; but, rather to his irritation, Bywaters thought it was an even better joke than he did. He got fifty dollars' allowance on it (not that he needed the damned fifty dollars, but them that had it never got it by throwing any away) by threatening to cancel the order on his new Duesenberg.

It looked like a Pullman car. And it turned out to use a bit more gas and oil than the Durant. But what the hell! If there was one thing he had plenty of that was it. While he was out burning it up in those twelve big-bore cylinders, back home that little old pump, going steady as the heart in his breast, was bringing up more. And at night while the car rested, and after he himself had been lulled to sleep by that sweet cradlelike rhythm, the pump worked on, rocket-a-bump, rocket-a-bump, rocket-a-bump . . .

One day the man who maintained the pump, on one of his periodical visits, happened to let drop something which suggested that both Jordan's and his neighbor's wells were drawing upon the same subterranean pool.

"You mean," cried Jordan with a white face, "you mean that son of a bitch is tapping onto my oil?"

What could he do about it? Nothing! Couldn't he go to law? He had got there first. Didn't a man have no rights? Couldn't they do something? Install a second pump? Replace this one with a bigger, stronger, faster one? Sink a thicker pipe? Christ, wasn't there nothing could be done to stop him, keep ahead of him, get it before he took it all?

But they didn't care, the oilmen. The same company (a Yankee outfit) had drilled both wells, his and his neighbor's. They were getting theirs on both sides of the fence, the sons of bitches. What the hell did they care which of them got more on his royalty check? It was all one and the same to them.

Jordan tried to visualize the lake of oil deep underground. It seemed to have shrunk. It had seemed bigger before, when he had thought of it as lying just under his own thirty acres, than it did now that he must think of it as extending also under his neighbor's forty-odd. Twelve acres more of it that damned Bywaters had than he had! To think there was a time when he could have bought him out at fifteen dollars an acre! A piddling six hundred dollars! Christalmighty, he spent more than that a week now. To be sure, at the time he didn't have six dollars cash money, much less six hundred, and wouldn't have spent it on Clarence Bywaters's forty acres of dust and erosion if he had had. It was enough to bring on heart failure when Jordan recalled that he had countered Bywaters's price by offering to sell out to him at ten an acre.

They had had to drill deeper on his neighbor's land. Did that mean that it was shallower on his side, that his oil was draining downhill into Bywaters's deeper pool? Was he just on the edge of it and Bywaters sitting in the middle? Since they had had to drill deeper that meant that his neighbor had a longer pipe. Jordan pictured the two of them underground, both sucking away, and the level of the pool dropping lower and lower, and suddenly his pipe made a sound like a soda straw makes at the bottom of the glass when the ice-cream soda is all gone. But his neighbor's pipe went on sucking greedily away.

The sound of his neighbor's pump, now that he knew it was pumping *his* oil, was like the steady drip of a leaky faucet: Jordan couldn't not hear it. Rocket-a-bump, rocket-a-bump, rocket-a-bump, all day long and into the night, growing louder and louder, drowning out nearer sounds, including that of his own pump.

Once Jordan's pump stopped. He was lying in bed one

night, sweating, tossing, the pounding of his neighbor's pump like a migraine headache, hating his wife for her deep untroubled sleep at his side, when suddenly his pump stopped. That was his own damned heart he heard, his pump had stopped. He leaped out of bed, ignoring his wife's sleepy, questioning whine, and dashed outdoors in his BVD's. It was going. Thank God, it was going. The relief was almost more than Jordan could stand. But wasn't it going slower, weaker? It seemed to be going slower. Had it reached the bottom and was it having to strain to draw up the last little bit? Or was it only that his heart was beating so fast?

From that time on the rocket-a-bump, rocket-a-bump, instead of lulling Jordan to sleep at night, kept him awake, listening, afraid it was going to stop, uncertain whether it was his own he was hearing or his neighbor's. He had to give up rocking in his rocking chair: the noise it made interfered with his listening. He sat very still, listening. He was afraid to go off for a ride in his car for fear his pump might stop while he was gone. Sometimes at night, when at last out of exhaustion he dropped off and momentarily ceased to hear the fevered rhythm of his own pulse drumming in his ear against his twisted and sweaty pillow, he awoke with a jerk, sure that his pump had stopped, that it was the other that he heard, and at such times as he bolted up in the darkness his heart gasped and gurgled as if it had drawn up the very last drop.

The bills for his new style of living began pouring in, bills of a size to take your breath away, in numbers like germs. Debts Jordan had always had, money to pay them with never before. The one was real, the other just paper, something in a bank. He lectured his wife and daughters on their extravagance. He reminded them how well they had always got by before without jewels and permanent waves. How much money a rich man needed!

146

Meanwhile that s.o.b. next door was really living high. Burning up the road in a Graham roadster. A blowout every weekend. Delivery vans from Ardmore and Oklahoma City pulling up to the door all day long. And his womenfolks going around bundled up in furs when it was a hundred and ten degrees in the shade, looking like an escaped zoo. He was not economizing. Whenever they met, Bywaters gave him such a glad hand and such a big fat possum-eating grin that the conviction grew on Jordan's mind that his neighbor was laughing at him. If Bywaters knew—and how could he not know?—that they were both pumping out of the same pool, it never fazed him. Which could only mean that he somehow knew he was getting the lion's share.

Jordan was not the only one to notice those fur coats, those delivery vans. Complaining that they were tackier now than when they were poor, his wife and daughters whined at him from morn till night. Clarence Bywaters now, his wife and daughters were dressed as women in their position ought to be. Were the Bywaters any better off than they were? And they would catalog the finery which Mrs. Bywaters and each of the Bywaters girls had worn to church that morning. As if Jordan hadn't seen! As if it wasn't him who was paying for every stitch of all those gladrags! How could he afford to deck out his own women when it was him who was outfitting Bywaters's like four grand duchesses?

Often poor Jordan chewed the bitter cud of that moment when his neighbor had offered to sell out to him. The scene was vivid in his mind. He saw Bywaters's furrowed brow, saw him stroke his stubbly chin, saw his head shake, heard him say, "It's a dog's life. Crops burning up. Soil all blown away. Cotton selling for nothing. If I could just raise the money I'd leave tomorrow. You know anybody that'll give me fifteen an acre?" Jordan had laughed.

Oh, how he wished he had it to do over again! Surely he could have raised six hundred dollars if he had only tried. He could have borrowed that on his own place. It already had a first lien on it, but he could have got a second. Oh, why had he let that golden opportunity slip? Then all seventy-two acres of that lake of oil would have been his, both those pumps his alone. These days to lay his hands on six hundred dollars all he had to do was reach in his pocket. He saw himself doing so. He saw Bywaters's face break into a grateful smile, felt the grateful pressure of his hand. His heart melted with pity for his neighbor, poor son of a bitch, and with the warmth of its own generosity. "California, here I come!" said Bywaters, hope shining like a rainbow through the tears brimming in his eyes. "Best of luck, ol' hoss," Jordan said. "I'll miss you." From this dream he was awakened by the throb of his neighbor's pump.

To wash the bitter taste from his mouth Jordan would take a pull at the bottle, drinking red whiskey now instead of white, his sole extravagance. Presently, despite himself, he would slip into another reverie. Rocking faster and faster as the figures mounted, he would calculate how much ahead he would be if his neighbor's pump was to break down, be out of commission for a week, ten days, two weeks. A month. Two months! Three! By then he was rocking so fast that when he caught himself and slowed down he was out of breath and panting, in a sweat. All he had succeeded in doing was in figuring how much his neighbor was making every minute. Then he would feel the hairs on the nape of his neck rise up and tingle as though someone was watching him.

Then Jordan knew he was in for it, and his heart seized with dread. For any misfortune wished upon another is a boomerang, it circles back and hits you. A man can't think one mean thought, not even in a whisper, not even

148

alone in a dark room at night or down in a cave deep in the earth, without Him hearing it and visiting it right back on you. Once a thought has been thought there is no calling it back. It goes out on the air like the radio waves, with the thinker's name all over it. He gets a whiff and says, "Who made that bad smell?" He looks down, right at you, and grabs you by the scruff of the neck and rubs your nose in your own mess.

So it was bound to happen. Try as he might to unwish the wish that his neighbor's pump might fail, Jordan went right on wishing it. So it was only a matter of time until his own broke down. Really. Not just a false alarm. And who knew for how long? Two weeks? Not likely! He had wished three months against Bywaters.

As is so often the case in such matters, for all his anxiety, Jordan was unaware of it when it befell. He had lain awake that night listening so intently to the hateful sound of his neighbor's pump that he didn't not hear his. Or maybe he fondly imagined that it was Bywaters's which had stopped, permitting him to fall asleep at last. The silence awoke him early next morning: steady, throbbing silence, and, in the background, Bywaters's pump going doubletime. He went out on the porch and looked. The beam hung down as if it had been pole-axed.

Jordan called the Company, his wife called the doctor. Keep him in bed and away from drink, the doctor advised; but he was no sooner gone than Jordan was out on the front porch rocking nervously and drinking steadily as he awaited the repairmen. It was midmorning before they showed up, nearly noon before the one sent for the replacement part got back.

"Have her going for you again in no time now, Colonel," they said.

But they fiddled and laid down their tools to talk and roll and smoke cigarettes and dawdled in the shade over their lunch and started looking at their watches half an hour before quitting time, and by then Bywaters's pump was going in jig time. So was Jordan in his rocker, until all of a sudden he came to a dead stop. He was still warm when they got to him but it was as if rigor mortis had set in while he was still alive. They had to pry him loose from that chair, and getting him into his coffin was like straightening a bent nail.

There is nothing on earth as dry as a handful of red Oklahoma dirt, though deeper down may lie an ocean of black gold. They crumbled their handfuls over Jordan Terry and shook their heads. A crying shame, said Jordan's lifelong friend and neighbor Clarence Bywaters as they were leaving the graveyard, a crying shame the poor son of a bitch had only lived to enjoy his wealth such a little while.

A Voice
from
the Woods

"Ssh! Listen," says my wife. "You hear? Listen."

"What?" says my mother.

"Hear what?" say I.

"Ssh! There. Hear it? An owl. Hooting in the daytime."

Then I do hear: a soft hollow note, like someone blowing across the lip of a jug: *hoo-oo, hoo-hoo-hoo; hoo-oo, hoo-hoo-hoo* . . .

A ghostly sound, defying location, seeming in successive calls to come out of the woods from all points of the compass. Near at hand one moment, far away and faint the next, barely audible, the echo of an echo. It is not an owl. Yet it cannot be what it is. Not here. So far from home. It comes again, this time seeming to sound not outside me but inside myself, like my own name uttered in a once-familiar, long-dead voice, and my mother says, "Owl? That's no owl. Why, it's a—"

"A mourning dove!" say I.

It is the sound, the solitary sound, save for the occasional buzz, like an unheeded alarm clock, of a locust, of the long hot somnolent summer afternoons of my Texas boyhood, when the cotton fields shimmered white-hot and in the black shade of the pecan trees bordering the fields the Negro pickers lay napping on their sacks and I alone of all the world was astir, out with my air rifle hunting doves I never killed, gray elusive ghosts I never could locate. I would mark one down as it settled in a tree (I remember the finicking way they had of alighting, as if afraid of soiling their feet), and would sneak there and stand listening, looking up into the branches until I grew dizzy and confused. I would give up and move on, and at my back the bird would come crashing out of the branches sounding its other note, a pained squeak, and wobble away in drunken flight and alight in another tree and resume its plaint. They favored cedars, at least in my memory, and cedars in turn favored burial grounds, so that I think of the dove's whispered dirge as the voice of that funereal tree. It would be one of those breathless afternoons when the sun cooked the resin from the trunks of pines and sweet-gums and the air was heavy, almost soporific with the scent. Heat waves throbbed behind the eyes. The fields were empty, desolate. High overhead a buzzard wheeled. The world seemed to have died, and in the silence the dove crooned its ceaseless inconsolable lament: *hoo-oo, hoo-hoo-hoo; hoo-oo, hoo-hoo-hoo . . .*

"A what? Mourning dove?" my wife says. "I never knew we had them here." *Here* being among the budding sugar maples and the prim starched white paper birches in the bustle and thaw of a crisp New England spring.

"I never knew you did either," says my mother. "What is a mourning dove doing way off up here?"

"What are you doing way off up here?" I say.

For my mother, too, has left Texas, lives out in Indianapolis. Now she has come on her annual visit to us.

We sit on the sun porch, rushing the season a bit. As always, we two have fallen to reminiscing of Blossom Prairie and our life there before my father's death, telling stories by the hour which both of us have heard and told so often now that it is the rhythm which stirs us more than the words, our tongues thickening steadily until the accent is barely intelligible to my Yankee wife, who listens amused, amazed, bewildered, bored, and sometimes appalled.

"Son, do you remember," my mother says, "the time the bank was held up?"

I am still listening to the dove, and I have to ask her what she said. But now she is listening to the dove and does not hear me.

"The time the bank was held up? No, I don't remember that. First time I ever heard of it."

"Hmm? What did you say? First time you ever heard of what?"

"Of the bank being held up. The bank in Blossom Prairie?"

"Really? Oh, you remember such funny things! Old Finus, that used to come around to the house every afternoon selling hot tamales. Why anybody should clutter up their memory with him, I don't know! Lord, I would never have given him another thought this side of the grave. And not remember the great bank robbery! You were old enough. You remember lots of things that happened long before that. I took you with me, and we saw the dead men lying on the sidewalk on the square. You've forgotten that?"

"Dead men? Lying on the sidewalk? On the square? What dead men?"

"The bank robbers. All shot dead as they came out of the bank. You don't remember?"

"What!" says my wife. "You took a child to see a sight like—"

"That's the kind of thing I remember! Not an old boy

who used to come around crying, 'Hot tamales!' Why, that was just about the biggest thing that ever happened in Blossom Prairie, I should think."

I open more cans of beer, and she drinks and sets down the can and wipes her lips and says, "Well, it was back in the bad old days. When lots of men were out of work and some of the young ones, who had all cut their teeth on a gun, took to living by it. The age of the great outlaws, when we had Public Enemy Number One, Two, Three. In our parts Pretty Boy Floyd was carrying on. And Clyde Barrow and Bonnie Parker."

"Did Clyde and Bonnie stick up the bank in Blossom Prairie?"

"No, no, it wasn't them. But it was in those days and times. No, the ones that stuck up the bank in Blossom Prairie—"

"Wait. Who was Pretty Boy Floyd?" asks my wife. "Who were Clyde Barrow and Bonnie Parker?"

"You never heard of them?" asks my mother, wiping away her mustache of suds.

"Now we will never get the story of the Blossom Prairie bank robbery," say I.

"Never heard of Clyde Barrow and Bonnie Parker? Never even heard of Pretty Boy Floyd?"

"Pretty Boy!" my wife laughs. "Pretty Boy!"

"Clyde Barrow," I say, "was a notorious outlaw, and Bonnie Parker his gun moll. They came out of West Dallas, the real low-down tough section of the town. They tore around sticking up banks and filling stations and honkeytonks, and between them shot and killed any number of bank tellers and gas-pump operators and law officers in Texas in the early thirties. We used to follow the exploits of Clyde and Bonnie in the newspapers every day, like keeping up with the baseball scores. We really cannot claim Pretty Boy Floyd. He was an Oklahoma hero."

"You're making fun," says my mother. "Well, no doubt they did a lot of bad things, but let me tell you, hon"— this to her daughter-in-law—"you can go back down there and out in the country and to this day you'll find a many an old farmer will tell you he was proud to give Pretty Boy Floyd a night's lodging when the law was hounding him down like a poor hunted animal, and more than likely they found a twenty-dollar bill under his breakfast plate after he had left the next morning. And he never got that nickname for nothing. Oh, he was a good-looking boy!"

"Well, what about the ones that held up the bank in Blossom Prairie?"

"He was a good-looking boy, too. All three of them were."

"She just never could resist an outlaw," I say.

The dove calls again, and my wife says, "What a sad, lonesome sound. I hope she doesn't come to nest around here. I wouldn't like to listen to that all day."

"As a matter of fact," says my mother, "as a matter of fact, I knew one of them. Travis Winfield, his name was. He was the leader of the gang. You wouldn't remember the Winfields, I don't suppose? Lived in that big old yellow frame house beyond the bridge out on the old McCoy road? A wild bunch, all of those Winfields, the girls as well as the boys, but good-looking, all of them, and Travis was the best-looking, and the wildest, of the lot. Well, anyway. One day when you were—oh, let's see, you must have been six or seven, which would make it—how old are you now, hon, thirty-eight?"

"Seven."

"Thirty-seven?"

"Yes'm."

"Are you sure?"

"I *was*. Aren't you?"

"Oh, you! Well, anyway, it was during the summer that

you had your tonsils and adenoids out. Remember? We were living at the time in Mr. Early Ellender's little cottage out on College Avenue. I had that little old Model-A Ford coupé that your daddy had bought me."

"Was there a college in Blossom Prairie?" my wife asks.

"No!"

"Well, you were just getting over that operation, and that's how you happened to be at home at the time and not off somewhere or other out of call. I remember I was fixing dinner when the telephone rang. . . . No, honey, there wasn't any college in Blossom Prairie. It was just a little bitty old place—though it was the county seat, and we all thought we were really coming up in the world when we left the farm and moved into town. It was so little that his daddy used to come home for his dinner every day. What you call lunch. . . . Well, the telephone rang and it was Phil. 'Hop in your car and come right down!' he said. 'They've just shot and killed three men robbing the bank!'"

"Then why was it called College Avenue? That doesn't make much sense."

"Don't ask me. I just grew up there."

"Well, but didn't it ever occur to you to wonder why they would call it that when there wasn't any—"

"Now, here is what had happened. These four men—"

"Three, you just a minute ago said."

"I said three were killed. These four men had been camping out down in Red River Bottom and— However, I better start with the woman. There was this woman, see. She had come into town about a month before. A stranger. She took a house, and she gave herself out to be a widow woman interested in maybe settling in the town and opening some kind of business with the money her husband had left her. And she had had a husband, all right, but she was no widow, nor even a grass widow. That came out at the trial. In fact, her husband showed up at the trial. When the judge sentenced her to eighteen years in the penitentiary this man stood up in the courtroom and said, 'Mildred! I'll still be waiting for you!' And she said, 'You'll wait a lot longer than any eighteen years!' And as they were taking her away he yelled, 'Mildred! Darling! I forgive you!' Meaning he forgave her for leaving him and running off with Travis. And that she-devil turned and told him I-can't-tell-you-what that he could do with his such-and-such forgiveness, right there in front of the judge and jury and the whole town and county. And still the poor fool did not give up but went round to the jailhouse and yelled up at the window of her cell until finally she came to the bars. And do you know what she told him was the one thing he could do that might win her back?— and this, you understand, would be after waiting for her to come out of the penitentiary for eighteen years. To get a gun and go shoot the one that had told on them to the law and had got the lover that she had run off with killed. However, it was not him that did it."

"That did what? Wait. I don't—"

"She was a cutter! Well, shortly after coming to town she went to the bank one day and opened an account. The very next day she was back and said she had changed her mind and wanted to draw her money out. They asked her why, and she said she had had her money in a bank once that had been held up, and she seemed to imply that that bank had looked a lot stronger than what she saw of ours. This piqued the manager, and he took her on a tour of the place to convince her that her money was safe with them, showing her all the strong vaults and the time locks and the burglar-alarm system and how it worked and whatnot. Besides, he said, there had never been any bank robberies in Blossom Prairie. So he convinced her, and she said she would let her money stay. After that she would come in every so often and make a deposit or a withdrawal, and she got to know the layout of the bank. She was making a map of it at home, and after each trip she would go and fill it in some more and correct any mistakes she had made in it. That way, too, she came to know when the big deposits were made by the business firms and the big-scale farmers and when there was always the most cash on hand in the bank.

"Meanwhile, she wasn't spending much time in that house in town. She told her neighbors—and of course they told everybody and his dog—that she still hadn't made up her mind to settle in Blossom Prairie and was looking over other spots around the county before deciding. She was seen on the road a lot, and she was a demon at the wheel. I was a pretty hot driver my own self, but—"

"Was! You still are. You scare me half to death."

"Well, that redheaded woman handled a car like no other woman and few men that I ever saw. In town she would spread her shopping over all the grocery stores so it wouldn't look like she was buying more food than a lone woman could eat, and she bought a good deal of bootleg liquor too, it came out later, and she would fill up the car and slip off down to Red River Bottom where Travis and his gang were camped out, though of course nobody knew that at the time. Whenever any squirrel hunter would happen to come up on them Travis kept out of sight, as he was the only local boy among them, and the other three made out that they were a hunting party too.

"Travis had been gone from home for some years, and everybody had pretty well forgotten him, except for maybe a couple of dozen girls who would have liked to but couldn't. Word would get back every now and again of some trouble he had gotten into and gotten himself out of. Now he had rounded up this gang and come back to rob the bank in his old home town. But though he had grown up there, he had to have that woman, or somebody, to draw him a map of the bank, for I don't suppose poor Travis had ever set foot in it in his life.

"All the while that he was holing up down there in the woods laying his plans Travis had living with him in that tent, and eating and drinking with him, one man who was in constant touch with the sheriff. He had told him all about that woman and about that map she was drawing of the bank and every little detail and switch in their plans. Imagine it? Living with three men for a whole month and letting on to be their friend, listening to them plan how they'll do this and do that to get the money and make their getaway, and knowing all the while that they were walking into a death trap that he himself had set, for pay, and that they were doomed to die as surely as if he himself had pulled the trigger on them? I'm not saying that what they were meaning to do was right, you understand. But can you just feature a skunk like that?

"I and Phil must have been just about the only people in town that didn't know the bank was set to be robbed that Monday morning. The sheriff had gone out and hired eight extra deputies, old country boys, good shots, squirrel hunters, and had them waiting, each with a thirty-thirty rifle, on the roofs of the buildings on each corner across the street from the bank, the old Ben Milam Hotel and the other, well, office buildings, stores downstairs on the street and doctors' and lawyers' offices upstairs, four stories high. The tellers in the bank had all been told not to put up any resistance but to give them what they asked for, to fill up their sacks for them, they'd have it all right back. The tip-off man was to wear something special. I seem to recall he wore a sailor straw hat, so they would recognize him and not shoot him.

"You remember, the bank in Blossom Prairie sits on the

northwest corner of the square. The street that goes out to the north, Depot Street, goes past the cotton compress and over the tracks and past the ice house and towards the river. That would be the street they would come in on. The one going out to the west went past your daddy's shop and over the creek and on out of town in the direction of Paris. Down this street that morning, headed towards the square, came a wagon loaded high with baled hay. On the wagon seat, dressed up in overalls and a twenty-five-cent hardware-store straw hat, sat Sheriff Ross Shirley, and under the seat lay a sawed-off pump shotgun. At twenty minutes to eleven he set his team in motion with a flick of the reins. A moment later a car came round the corner and pulled up alongside the curb, and four men got out and ducked into the bank. As soon as they were inside, the sheriff says 'Come up' to his team, and up on the roof-tops the rifle barrels poke over the walls and point down, followed by the heads of those eight deputies. The woman was driving, and she stayed in the car, keeping the engine idling. The wagon came down the street towards her, rattling over those old *bois-d'arc* paving bricks, until it got to just a little ways in front of the car. There suddenly the left rear wheel flew off the axle, the load of hay came tumbling down, scattering clear across the street, bales bouncing and breaking apart, the street completely blocked. The woman in the car made a sudden change in plans. She threw into reverse and backed around the corner into Depot Street, thinking that now, instead of going out by the Paris road, they would have to cross the square and go out by the southwest. Then she sees ahead of her a man fixing a flat tire on a big delivery van out in the middle of the street halfway down the block. This meant, she thought, that she would have to cut diagonally across the square, through the traffic and around the plaza and out by the southeast corner. She didn't know it, but they had her cut off there, too. In another minute or so the men burst out of the bank carrying the sacks.

"The moment they stepped out the door it began to rain bullets on them. Those that were on the square at the time said it sounded like a thunderclap had broken overhead. You couldn't count the separate shots, they said. The bullets chewed holes in the cement sidewalk. The men must have all died in the first volley, but the deputies poured another round and then another into them as they went down. The fourth man had fallen a step behind, deciding not to trust everything to that sailor straw hat, maybe thinking they would just as soon not pay that reward, and when the noise broke he dove back into the bank. He had cast a quick look up above as he came out, and that woman in the car must have seen it. In any case, when he didn't come out with the rest a thousand things that she must have noticed at the time and shaken off suddenly added up like a column of figures in her mind. She didn't even try to run. She jumped out of the car and up onto the curb, swooped down and pried the pistol from the still-clutching hand of one of the bandits, and stepped over the body into the bank. By then the sheriff was one step behind her. He grabbed her and took the gun away from her and held her until help came. She was more than he could manage alone. They said it was all four big strong men could do to keep her from getting at that one and clawing his eyes out, and then when they dragged her outside she broke away and threw herself on the body in the doorway, crying, 'Travis! Travis! Speak to me, Travis!' They had taken her away, and taken away the informer too and locked him up for his own protection by the time we got there, but the bodies were still lying on the sidewalk where they had fallen."

"Taking a little six-year-old child to see a sight like that!" my wife says, shaking her head.

"It was a terrible sight to see. Three strong young men cut off in the very Maytime of life, shot down like mad dogs before they even knew what was happening to them. I was sorry I had come. I wasn't going to look any closer. I tried to back out of the crowd. Then Phil said, 'My Lord! Why, ain't that one there that Winfield boy, Travis?' Oh, what a funny feeling came over me when I heard Phil say that!"

"Why, had you known him pretty well?"

"Yes. In fact—well, in fact, I had gone with Travis Winfield for a time, before I married your daddy."

"You had!"

"In fact, Travis Winfield had once asked me to marry him. He was not a bad boy then. Wild, yes, but not mean, not any gangster. I—I thought about it awhile before I turned him down. That stung him, and he didn't ask me a second time. I was just as glad. Oh, he was a good-looking boy! I don't know what I might have said a second time. Well, he had quickly forgotten about me and I had gone out with other boys and in time had met and married Phil, your daddy, and wasn't ever sorry that I had. But I want you to know I felt mighty queer standing there looking down at poor Travis—he was still handsome, even there in the dirt and all bloodied—lying on the common sidewalk with people staring at him, and thinking of that wild woman who had loved him so and had shared his wild life and now been dragged off to prison, and I was glad to have you there to hold on to. It was a comfort to me then to have my own child to hold on to his hand."

Silence falls, and in it the dove utters again it dolorous refrain.

"My daddy and my brothers disapproved of Travis Winfield. I think—apart from the fact that I was infatuated with his reputation for wildness, and his good looks —I think I probably went with him mainly just to devil my brothers a bit, let them all worry over me a little maybe, at least give them some reason for all that concern over my reputation. I don't believe I was every really serious about him, and I never thought he was serious about me, partly because there were already lots of stories of other girls he hadn't been serious over. So I was taken by surprise when he asked me that day to marry him. I told him I would give him my answer next week. I knew then what it would be, but I suppose I wanted a week of thinking of accepting what I knew I was going to turn down.

"You remember, honey, out back of my old home that little family graveyard where all my folks are buried? It was there that Travis Winfield proposed to me. I said to meet me there again next Sunday and I would give him my answer. I remember waiting for him to come. You know how still it can be on a farm on a Sunday afternoon. The only sound for miles around as I sat there waiting for him was the cooing of a dove. I sat there thinking, I'm going to turn him down, of course, but what if I was not to? What if I was to say yes? What would my life be like?

"There are people just born for trouble, you know; Travis Winfield was one of them. It was written all over him in letters like headlines. Wild. Stubborn. Headstrong. Full of resentment against those who had all the things he didn't have. Proud. Vain. Believing the world owed him a living for the sake of his pretty face. No one woman could ever hope to hold him for long. After a while she wouldn't even want to keep on trying, unless she was an utter fool. But certainly life with Travis wouldn't be dull. It would be different from life on the farm, or in Blossom Prairie in a bungalow that had to be swept out and dusted every day.

"But I knew what I was going to say, and I said it. And maybe Travis wasn't sorry to hear it. Maybe during the week he had begun to wish he hadn't asked me. Most likely it was just his pride. He wasn't used to having a girl say no to anything he wanted. In any case, he didn't ask me again, and I was glad he didn't. He just gave me a hot look and turned and left. After he was gone I sat there a long time listening to the mourning dove. I never saw him again until that day on the square. It's years now since I even thought of Travis Winfield. It was hearing that mourning dove that brought it all back to my mind."

We sit listening for some time to its call. Then something alarms it, and though we do not see it, we hear the thrashing of its wings among the branches and its departing cry.

"Who did shoot the one who told?" I ask.

"Oh, yes, him. The trustees of the bank voted him a big reward, but he never got to spend it. They found him a week later floating in the river, though it was a wonder, with all the lead he had in him. It was generally known to be the work of that Winfield tribe, but they could never prove it. Never tried any too hard, I don't suppose."

I make a move to rise, but seeing her face I sit down again. Brushing back a strand of her cotton-white hair, my mother says, "Aren't people funny? There in his blood lay Travis, whom I had forgotten, dead, and deservedly so, I suppose, if any man deserves it. There was I, happy, with a good, loving husband and a decent home and a smooth, even life ahead of me and my own child's hand in mine. And yet, thinking of that redheaded woman—even then on her way to prison—I felt, well, I don't know what else to call it if not jealousy. Isn't that crazy? What did she have? Nothing, less than nothing, and I had everything. It only lasted a moment, you understand, yet it comes back to me even now, and if it wasn't jealousy, then I don't know what else to call it."

The
Human Fly

IN LATE August 1935, this advertisement appeared in our local weekly, the New Jerusalem, Texas, *Lariat and Northern Bee*:

GRIPPO
The Human Fly
He Defies the Law of Gravity
! ! ! ! ! !
On Saturday, October 5
The Great
GRIPPO
Relying Entirely Upon the Strength of His Own Two Hands
Unassisted and Unprotected by
Ropes, Belts, Spurs, Nets, or
Any Safety Devices
Whatsoever
Will Attempt to Scale the Walls and Tower of the
CANAAN COUNTY COURTHOUSE
(Eight Stories Tall)
! ! ! ! ! !
See Grippo Risk Life and Limb in His
DEATH-DEFYING ASCENT
! ! ! ! ! !

Can He Do It
? ? ? ?
Grippo Boasts
"The Building I Can't Climb Has Not Been Built!"
! ! ! ! ! !
Be On Hand for Whatever *May Be Fall*
! ! ! ! ! !
WARNING
Persons who have been Advised by Doctor
or Physician to Avoid Excitement are
Hereby Cautioned that they Attend at
THEIR OWN RISK
! ! ! ! ! !
This ad is your ticket of admission

My over-forty readers will surely remember the human
flies. Younger ones, your parents will tell you that the
human fly was a craze, like flagpole sitting, marathon
dancing, of that desperate period the Great Depression.

Things were as desperate with us in New Jerusalem,
Texas, as with others elsewhere in those times, and maybe
a little more so; but we had no marathon dancing, no
flagpole sitters. And although we had, in our courthouse,
the building for it, we never expected to attract to us anything so exciting as a human fly.

New Jerusalem, it must be admitted, was and is rather
off the beaten track. The town was not as big in 1935 as
it had been in 1905, before Egyptian cotton cut so disas-
trously into the market for our one crop. An Egyptian
will pick cotton for less pay even than a Negro. New Jerusalem had not grown as our grandfathers, the builders of
our courthouse, so confidently envisaged it would.

So when in 1935, in the very depths of the Depression,
our local Chamber of Commerce received a letter from
this Grippo offering, upon a certain guarantee, to come to

166

New Jerusalem and scale our courthouse, it seemed a
blessing fallen from heaven. That year we seemed to have
hit rock bottom. What the national Depression had left
us, our regional dust storms had taken from us. Trade was
at a standstill, with merchants leaning in their doorways
or staring out their windows over the piles of unsold goods,
men long out of work beginning to mutter their resentment, dangerously in need of some distraction. Our courthouse was just made for a human fly. People would flock
to see him. The day he came to town would see much
money change hands. To a man the C of C voted to accept
his offer, assessed themselves, and raised for Grippo his
minimum purse. This was rumored to be as much as one
thousand dollars, which was a lot more money in those
days than it is now, and in New Jerusalem still is. In return,
as a matter of form, Grippo, or his heirs, agreed to waive
any claim upon the town in the event that he should, while
performing on municipal property, suffer any mishap.

During the five weeks that ticket-ad ran, the *Lariat and
Northern Bee,* as I, its owner, editor, and publisher, can
avouch, sold more copies than at any period in its previous,
or subsequent, history. "California" Stan Reynolds might
say he wasn't going, but he was the only person in New
Jerusalem, or in all of Canaan County, who wasn't. Which
was right where Stan always stood vis-à-vis his home
town on everything: out in left field all by himself. Stan's
cantankerousness and lack of any civic sense—which is
putting it mildly—was what had earned him his nickname, "California." That was meant to be derisive. Stan
had been telling us for years how he couldn't wait to
shake the dust of New Jerusalem off his heels; at last one
day he announced his imminent departure for California,
the land of his dreams. In a small community it is a great
mistake to say a thing like that and then not do it. Espe-

cially if like Stan, in making the announcement, you burn all your bridges behind you by telling everybody exactly what you've always thought of them. Stan got as far as Paris, forty-seven miles west of here, on that and a couple of subsequent flights, and that was as close as Stan ever got to California, or ever would now that, as he himself publicly phrased it, he had saddled himself with a wife, now that there were two kids with another on its way, now that he was pushing thirty, and now that hard times were upon us, it looked like, to stay. So we called him, in mockery of his blighted dreams, "California," and he called us—whatever he could lay tongue to. He was the town crab and killjoy, and when he said he wasn't going he meant it. But if he thought he would be missed he was much mistaken. Everybody was tickled to hear that he would not be on hand to spoil the fun with his sour remarks the day Grippo came to town.

During the five weeks of mounting excitement from the time of the announcement to the great day itself the town took a fresh look at its courthouse. In the speculation that then went on about which face of the building Grippo would choose for his assault, the curbstone attorneys who occupied the benches around the courthouse lawn split into four parties each of which thought the other three were all plain lunatics, although the building was and is exactly the same on all four sides. During that period, as a contribution to the general interest aroused by the forthcoming event, the paper, drawing for material upon the files of the *Northern Bee* (which preceded the *Lariat*), ran a series of articles on the construction, architecture, and history of the courthouse. While doing research for an obituary this past week, we have had the occasion to re-read that series. Briefly, what we said at the time was this.

The culture of small Southern towns like ours, we said, had been aptly called a Courthouse Culture. Certainly our courthouse, with its majestic steeple, visible on a clear day for forty miles in any direction, dominated New Jerusalem, despite the fact that it did not, as in many, if not most, Southern towns, occupy the center of the public square, but sat instead a block north of there in a spacious square of its own planted in leafy oaks and tall pecan trees. Constructed throughout of native Texas limestone, pitted like a Swiss cheese with impressions of marine fossils from the Jurassic and Pleistocene epochs, originally white, now mellowed to a pleasing soft cream color, the building had been begun in 1859 with the laying of the corner-stone. Interrupted by the War and the Reconstruction period, construction was resumed in 1878, completed and the building formally dedicated with appropriate ceremonies still remembered by some of our senior citizens, in 1882.

The style of architecture we labeled Colonial Gothic, a characterization which the passage of years has brought no need to revise.

Originally the basement floor, now the county free schoolbook depository, had housed the prisoners awaiting trial in the courtrooms overhead. By 1885, however, the county crime rate having exceeded expectations, need was felt for more spacious quarters, and the present four-story jailhouse was erected on its site a block to the west. The ground floor, raised some ten feet off the ground, and reached by broad flights of stone steps on all four sides, each leading to arched double doors eighteen feet in height, was square in plan, buttressed at the corners. The second floor duplicated, on a one-quarter-reduced scale, the first. From the second floor the windowless tower rose one hundred and sixteen feet, exclusive of the weathervane, for an overall height of one hundred and sixty-eight feet. On each of the tower's four sides was a round white clock face three feet in diameter. Above the clock was an open lookout. Above the lookout the tower terminated in a tapered cupola which housed the clock bell.

The clock bell, which on still days could be heard and the strokes counted up to ten miles away, with its bass, even somewhat solemn, but distinctly musical note, tolled every quarter hour beginning at six a.m. and going on until midnight, chiming four times for the quarter past, eight for the half, twelve for the three quarters, sixteen before the hour, and then the hour. This, the *Lariat and Northern Bee* informed its readers, added up to a total 877 chimes per day, 6139 per week, 26,310 per month—taking thirty days as the average month—and finally, the staggering figure of 320,105 chimes per year!

We omitted in our series to count the number of steps of the stairway inside the tower mounting to the lookout above the clock—and not being as young and spry now as we were then, we must beg to be excused from supplying the omission! But we did remind our readers that the stairway was there, open to the public admission-free, whereupon all of Canaan County, always excepting "California" Stan Reynolds, of course, made the climb, many of them, although native-born, for the first time. From the lookout the view over the flat, bare prairies which surround us is extensive in all directions on a clear day. All who made the ascent and looked to earth from that dizzying height roundly declared that nothing, not even a thousand dollars, could induce them to attempt to scale it with nothing but their own two hands. There were some then who opposed permitting even the Great Grippo to make the trial.

To arrive at the courthouse grounds by the hour they did on that Saturday morning, the fifth of October, some of the country people must have been traveling in their horse-drawn wagons since late the previous afternoon. They had begun to gather there by the light of the moon. By the time the clock sounded its first note of the day the lawn was already thronged. Cars with license tags from four surrounding counties were to be seen. Market Square as well as the public square being by then full, those arriving after six were obliged to take parking space wherever they could find it, some in residential streets as far distant as a mile's walk. In the public square bargain sales were announced in loud paint on the show windows of every store. Needless to say, these would open their doors for business only after Grippo's performance, as until then nobody would be doing any shopping, and the storekeepers and their employees were as eager as everybody else to see the show. By the time the clock struck seven the town, except for the courthouse lawn, was everywhere deserted and still. A thief could have walked off with the whole place unopposed, if he could have resisted the desire to see the human fly himself.

All eyes that day were turned steadily skywards. Indeed, for some time afterwards New Jerusalem and Canaan County, being accustomed in the pursuit of its ordinary daily occupations, such as plowing, cottonpicking, sweeping house, scrubbing clothes, et cetera, to an earth-inclined posture, was to suffer cricks in the neck in the proportions of an epidemic.

Shortly before eight o'clock a man wearing an aviator's leather helmet strapped underneath his chin and large dark-tinted goggles so that his face was almost entirely hidden appeared at the edge of the crowd and commenced working his way through it.

"Mister," one small boy mustered the courage to ask, "are you Grippo, the human fly?"

"The Great Grippo," replied the man in a husky voice, and to the *ah-hah*s of its party and the *ugh*s of the other three, strode to the east face of our courthouse, which was the first one he came to, and without wasting a second in studying the building but as if he had been born and raised in its shadow, proceeded to climb it. Those who had been waiting for him on the other sides hastened around to the chosen one, and the crowd thereupon became so dense that people standing close to one another had to take turns drawing breath. Small children and many not so small were hoisted to their fathers' and even to their mothers' shoulders.

"No! No!" a woman screamed. "I don't want to see it! Take me home!" A large woman she was, and when she fainted five men were needed to carry her off.

Grippo began by leaping from the ground and grasping a window ledge and hauling himself up to it. From there he stretched across to the next window and the next, going towards the door. He let himself down onto the porch and opened one half of the door back to the porch rail. He climbed the rail and straddled the door and shinnied up its edge like a monkey up a pole to the top of it. From there with the greatest of ease he hoisted himself to the roof.

Pausing only to fetch his breath, Grippo assaulted the second story. This he elected to scale by way of the drainpipe affixed to its southeast corner. It took him just five minutes by the clock overhead, but it seemed to all below much longer. Twice he lost his grasp and slipped downwards. This was no doubt a part of his act, but the crowd let out a gasp and on both occasions another woman passed out and had to be removed. The scariest moment came when, hauling himself over the edge of the roof, he slipped and hung dangling from the gutter in midair, the snap of his chin strap popping open and the flaps hanging loose. Then in a piercing voice a woman screeched, "Get

that man down from there! Get him down, I say, before
he falls and kills hisself before our very eyes!"

When Grippo had gained the second-story roof he stood
up and gave himself a shake and rested for some moments
to catch his breath, panting deeply. Among the crowd
down on the ground, meanwhile, breathing went suspended. Their gaze now elevated several notches, they
studied the lofty tower, all asking themselves how Grippo
meant to meet its daunting challenge. Now came the day's
real trial. The building he could not climb might not have
been built, but how did Grippo mean to scale those nearly
one hundred feet of perpendicularity, its blank surface unbroken but for the courses of gargoyles spaced at intervals
of some twelve or fifteen feet?

Grippo took off his shoes and socks and rolled up his
trousers and began walking up the wall like a fly. A gasp
of amazement ran through the crowd.

"It's not true!" a woman shouted. "I don't believe it!
I'm going home!"

How? How was Grippo doing it? He was doing it, the
realization dawned, relying on those Swiss-cheese-like fos-
sil holes in the stone for finger- and toeholds!

"Yawl can stay and watch if you want to but I'm going
home!" the same woman as before shouted.

Grippo did not go straight up. Searching ahead for
holes big enough to hook a finger or a toe in, he was often
forced to veer from his path to one side or the other, even
to descend and strike out on a fresh route, so that he
crisscrossed the entire face of the structure—very much
the way a fly climbs. Thus he was twenty minutes in gain-
ing the relative safety of the first gargoyle, upon whose
neck he sat for a well-earned five-minute rest. Then could
be seen the toll his climb was taking. The knees of his
trousers were torn open and his knees scraped raw and

red. Hanging as he did sometimes by a mere two fingertips in those jagged and sharp-edged holes, the punishment to them could be imagined.

"I can't stand it any more! I'm going home where I belong!" that same woman yelled.

After his rest Grippo's rate of climb was slower, and by the time he reached his second gargoyle it was almost nine by the clock. His rest at that station was a long one. It was a stone goat upon whose neck he sat this time, and it seemed to be bucking and trying to throw him off, so deep was his breathing. To the watchers on the ground the tower appeared to have grown in height and people were saying now that Grippo would never make it to the top.

At last he rose and faced the wall again and resumed his climb. One foot higher he lost his grip and fell. The crowd's cry died away on a vast sigh of relief as he caught the gargoyle in his descent. The jolt of his fall and its sudden arrest popped his helmet off and with it his goggles and sent them flying through the air. It was then in the general hush, broken only by the hysterical sobs of various women, that Mrs. Ernestine Reynolds, pear-shaped with her third child, cried out, "My Lord it's Stan!"

And my Lord she was right. It was. The Great Grippo was none other than our own "California" Stan Reynolds, in his desperation to escape from the home town he hated trying to climb his way out up the courthouse tower. The plump of two thousand hearts high in hopes sinking in sudden disappointment could almost be heard.

"Grippo my foot! Don't Grippo me!" Ernestine was shouting at her neighbors trying to persuade her and themselves that she must be mistaken. "I reckon I know my own husband when I see him—the crazy fool! Stan! Stanley Reynolds! What do you think you're doing? Come down from there! You hear me, Stan? Get down from there before you fall and break your neck! A fine fix that would

leave me in, wouldn't it! Children, hush your crying! Stan!
You— Oh! Watch out!" And she went green around the
gills.

For in struggling to haul himself onto the gargoyle
Stan's hold had slipped and he now hung only by his hands
with his feet kicking free in space.

"Run get a rope, somebody!" a man yelled.

"A rope! A rope! Run get a rope!" cried several all at
once.

Mr. McKinney, of McKinney's Hardware, waved his
store keys above his head, croaking to get himself noticed.
The keys were passed to the rear of the crowd and someone
set off running for the square. By the time the man got
back with the coil of rope Stan had succeeded in pulling
himself up and was once again sitting astraddle of the stone
goat. Now that he was about to be rescued, having spoiled
the day for all, mutters were heard that it would serve Stan
right if he fell and broke his neck. A party of five volunteers ran into the courthouse carrying the rope. In the
empty, high-ceilinged hallways their heavy footsteps could
be heard, then could be heard no more as they started up
the tower.

Stan must have heard them on the stairs inside going
past the point where he sat perched. Whereupon he stood
up and began again more determinedly than ever crawling
up the wall. Shouts from the crowd went up of, "Sit still!
Stay where you're at! Wait a second! They're coming with a
rope!" and from Ernestine the cry, "Oh! Just wait till I get
you home!" But Stan had climbed that high and could see
above him the attainment of all his dreams. He was determined to go the whole way and claim his prize—which was,
to spit in the faces of all those below him and then never
see them again. When the men of the rescue party appeared
in the lookout and dropped their rope, Stan continued on
his way, climbing up alongside it.

175

That was around half past nine. By ten Stan had gained two more gargoyles and was a little less than half-way to the top. It was an exhibition of frantic determination and mad bravery, and throughout it the crowd's mood had changed. At first, its hopes for a good time dashed, disgusted with being duped and boiling with indignation—a mob rather than a crowd—it was bent on having its own out of "California" Stan as soon as he was let back down to earth. But as Stan inched his way upwards, clinging for life by his fingertips, slipping and nearly falling and bringing every heart into every mouth at every moment, it began to dawn upon them that they were in fact seeing what they had come to see: a man scale the courthouse; and that if it was excitement they wanted they were getting not less but more out of watching an amateur, someone like themselves, do it, than they could have gotten out of watching a professional human fly. Nobody cheered: Stan had made himself too unpopular for that, and it could not be overlooked that that stubborn perseverance was the measure of his hatred of them all. Still it had to be admitted that what he was doing took nerve.

By eleven o'clock nerve was all the man was going on, and when finally he struggled to yet another of those stone billygoats it was plain to all that he had gone as high as he was going to go. Still he would not come down. Even after it must have been clear to Stan that he could go no higher but must give up and come down, he clung to his hard-won height, stubbornly ignoring the rope that dangled by his side, his wife who pled with him, threatened him, cursed him, and cried. Goaded by that hard-dying dream of his, or by the prospect of defeat, descent, he tried again, dragged himself up the wall another foot, then clung to it, unable to go up, unwilling to come down.

The rescue party in the lookout could be heard pleading with him. "Aw, come on, Stan, grab the rope. Please, Stan!

Grab the rope, won't you, Stan?" Down on the ground women wailed and shrieked while men called up, "We're not mad at you, Stan, hear? Nobody's going to hurt you when you get down. Just grab the rope. Please!"

The clock struck twelve. Sixteen solemn chimes and then the long slow counting of the hour. The final stroke died away. A spasm of despair followed by a shudder of surrender passed over the man clutching at the wall and he beat his head against the stone. Then he turned and let go and reached for the rope. And missed it and fell sixty-six feet to the roof of the second story.

The thousand women present let out a single scream, and still one heard the thud as the falling man struck the roof. Even those who managed to get their hands over their ears before he hit still heard inside their heads the heavy sickening thud, and felt it in every cell of their bodies.

He ought to have been instantly killed, but as a matter of fact, he survived—helplessly crippled, to be sure, but still miraculously alive. Despite some eleven operations over the years, all paid for by the community he so despised, he remained permanently bedridden and immobilized, requiring even to be fed, a duty which his wife conscientiously fulfilled, although her patient was not noted for a cheerful disposition.

The event has remained vivid in local memory, and often, hearing the clock strike the hour, New Jerusalemites pause at their play or at their busy chores to recollect for a moment those desperate hours it tolled that earlier day.

In October 1945, under "Ten Years Ago This Week," and again in October 1955, under "Twenty Years Ago This Week," the *Lariat and Northern Bee* reprinted its original account of that day when, as Grippo the Human Fly, Stan attempted to scale the courthouse tower, preserving unrevised in the interest of historical accuracy its concluding observation that he was not expected to live. Stan died in the little cottage provided for him near the jailhouse and we buried him just last week—it was his obituary I have lately had to write—after thirty-three years as a ward of the town. Anyone who supposes he was grateful for our charity not only didn't know Stan, he doesn't know human nature.

Some readers may, like ourself, be intrigued to know how many times the town clock chimed over that period. 10,563,465.

The Last
of
the Caddoes

I

By THE shores of the Red River, in Texas, lived a boy named Jimmy Hawkins, who learned one day to his surprise that he was, on his father's side, part Indian. Until then Jimmy had always thought he was just another white boy.

A curious reluctance had kept Jimmy's mother from ever telling him about his Indian blood. She had felt it from the time he first began to question her about himself, about the family. She shied away from it warily, almost as though in fear. This was very silly of her, of course. Just childishness. Some old bogeyman left over from her early childhood, nothing more. She had never seen a live Indian in her life. The savages, even in Texas, had long since been pacified, not to say exterminated. Being afraid of Indians in those days and times, when the only ones left were celluloid Indians, Saturday-matinee horse-opera Indians! *Ugh. How. Me big chief Squat-in-the-*

179

Mud. Heap big medicine. Ridiculous! It was quite plain that what she really felt was not fear at all, it was in fact a touch of jealousy, possessiveness. For it was not she but his father from whom the child got his Indian blood, and obviously she was jealous of that part of him, small as it was, that was alien to her. Not that this was not equally silly of her, of course. Not that the Indian in himself was not equally alien to her husband. Certainly he would never try to use this bond to draw the boy closer to himself, away from his mother. There was really no reason for it. And that was it, precisely. That explained entirely why Mrs. Hawkins, and, following her lead, Mr. Hawkins, had let their Jimmy reach the age of twelve without ever mentioning this trifle about himself: there was no reason to.

Yet all the while Jimmy's mother felt she really perhaps ought to just mention it. There were times, indeed, when it was as though she were being urged from all sides to tell him, reproached for her silence, even almost commanded to speak out without further delay. "But what on earth difference does it make?" she would argue. "Nowadays what difference does it make? None whatever." Though in fact it might have made a great difference to Jimmy. The boy was simply crazy about Indians: read about nothing else, dressed himself up as one, made himself beadwork belts, sewed his own moccasins; his mother might have guessed that to be able to claim he was part Indian would have pleased him as nothing else could. "But it's only the tiniest little fraction," she would rejoin. "Hardly enough to count." Or, again, "It isn't as if I had deliberately not told him. Heavens! Why on earth would I do that? What's it to me, one way or the other? The subject has simply never come up, that's all. If it ever should, why then, of course . . ." Just who it was she was arguing with at these times she never knew.

It came out unexpectedly one day when they were having one of their rows. Lately it had gotten so all they ever did, it seemed, was fuss and quarrel. Jimmy was passing through a difficult phase. Going on thirteen now, and feeling new powers stirring within him, he was forever testing his strength, trying his mother, seeing just how far he could go, how much he could get away with. This one was their third fight in two days. Jimmy had done something he knew not to do, had been scolded and punished, and had turned sullen and defiant. His punishment would end, he was told, when he confessed he had been bad and said he was sorry; the set of his jaw proclaimed that he had vowed he would sooner die. He could be very stubborn. He was getting to be more than a match for his mother, as he well knew: too big for her to switch any more—the very threat had begun to sound absurd—almost too big for his father to correct; and he soon reduced her to that frazzled state where, as she would say, she didn't know what to do. He grew bolder and more impudent until at last he said something so sassy she slapped his face. This made dart from Jimmy's black eyes two poisoned arrows of hatred. "Oh!" cried his mother, pierced by his look, "I don't know what gets into you at times like this!" Then before she knew it: "It must be the Indian in you coming out."

Jimmy instantly forgot his burning cheek. The Indian in him! Did she mean it? Real Indian? Which tribe? What part Indian was he? How long had this been known? Why had she never told him before?

But his mother had already told him more than she ever meant to. "You get it," she said dryly, "from your father, not me." To her surprise, and her chagrin, she found herself trembling, positively seething with anger. She felt somehow as though she had been tricked into letting it out. What was most exasperating was to find herself so vexed over a mere trifle. But what she felt was not altogether anger, and she knew it. One of her heartstrings had just been tied tight in a hard little knot of fear.

Jimmy's antics, meanwhile, did nothing to soothe her temper. His disobedience, his mother's displeasure, the sentence of punishment he was still under all forgotten, he was circling round and around her doing an Indian war dance. Brandishing an invisible tomahawk, he stamped his feet, ducked his head, then flung it back, all the while patting his mouth as he whooped, "Wah wah wah wah wah wah—" Until, shaking with rage, she hissed at him, "Little savage! Treat your mother with no more consideration than a wild savage! Well, that's just what you are! So act like one, that's right! Be proud of yourself for it!" Then she broke down in tears and ran sobbing from the room.

Thus, not until he was twelve, almost thirteen, and then only by accident (or so it seemed at the time), did Jimmy Hawkins learn that he was part Indian. And that that was the part his mother blamed for all she disliked in him.

II

How BIG a part? Which tribe? These questions, and others, Jimmy did not again put to his mother, eager as he was for an answer to them—not after her angry outburst. His hurt pride would not let him.

She had said he got it from his father, so Jimmy went to him. But he checked himself long before he got there. Not much pondering upon the matter was needed to make Jimmy even less willing to question his father than he was to question his mother. More Indian by half than he, his father had connived at, or at the very least had acquiesced in, keeping from his son the knowledge of his Indian ancestry. There was a name for men like his father, and a punishment decreed for them. His father was a renegade, and so without further ado Jimmy drummed him out of their tribe—whichever that might prove to be.

To be an Indian, even if only in part, was to Jimmy so glorious a fate it was impossible for him to imagine anyone feeling differently. But any lingering doubts he may have had about how differently his mother felt were soon dispelled. For although she had meant never to mention it— unless, that is to say, it just came up by itself, of course— once it was out and there was no taking it back, she found herself saying again and again, whenever he goaded her to it, which was often enough as the warfare between them went on, "That's the Indian in you coming out, that's what that bit of deviltry is. Little savage!" Though each time she said it it seemed to draw tighter that hard little knot in her heart.

And it was no sooner said than something awful began to happen. Something truly sinister. Something quite uncanny and even unbelievable, and yet precisely the sort of thing that might have been expected. Indeed, it now seemed to have been a premonition of this very thing that had kept her from ever speaking out before. Overnight Jimmy began to look like an Indian. He really did. What made this sudden transformation the more uncanny was that, strictly speaking, he looked no more like an Indian than he ever had, or ever would for that matter, with his corn-silk hair and pale, almost white eyebrows and lashes, his fair, not to say pallid, skin. His only feature that might have been Indian was his glittering black eyes—brown, actually, but a brown so dark, especially being set in that pale face, as to be really black. Yet all the same he really did begin to look like an Indian—more so every day—more so each time he was reproached with being one. More sullen and sly: more Indian.

It had certainly made a change in him: Jimmy could

see it for himself. And no wonder. For although it may have come out accidentally, the revelation that he was an Indian found him already prepared to be one. He knew all there was to know about Indians. All his reading, ever since he learned to read, had been about the Indians, and in the accounts of the wars between them and the white settlers he had always taken their side. Now at last he knew why. They had been calling to him, blood calling to blood.

The things about himself that Jimmy had not understood before were explained now. His outbursts of temper, his touchy pride, his moods of contrariness, his impulses of cruelty, the stubborn streak that so irritated his mother: his Indian blood not only accounted for all these, it absolved him from blame for them. If he behaved sometimes like a little savage it was because he was a little savage. It was not his fault. He was what he was. He felt a burden of guilt lifted from him. He was through forevermore with apologizing for himself. It was not his fault that he was part Indian. He could not change that. He could not have done anything about it even if he had wanted to.

Being an Indian was not going to be all fun then. It never had been: this Jimmy knew from his reading; to be one in his day and time was harder than ever, it seemed. Situated where he was, cut off from his people, not even knowing yet who his people were, he was alone, surrounded by the enemy. He would need to be very crafty, very cunning, very wary. He would need to tread softly. He would have to sleep always with one eye open. He would need to grow up very fast. At his age an Indian boy was already training to be a brave.

He no longer joined in childish games. It did not befit his new dignity. To be an Indian was a serious responsibility. He seldom smiled, never laughed any more. He comported himself with the gravity of a sachem, spoke with the sententiousness of one of Fenimore Cooper's sagamores. He exulted inwardly to see that his new disdainful silence was more exasperating to his parents and his schoolteachers than open defiance had ever been. When stung by one of his mother's slurs upon his Indian blood, he betrayed none of his resentment; he stored these up with Indian patience, all to be repaid with interest one day.

Meanwhile the more he brooded upon it the more he resented never being told that he was what he was. And who knew how much longer he might have been kept in ignorance? Had she not lost her temper that day and let it slip, his mother might never have told him. The prospect of this appalled Jimmy. When thought of that way it was not just the pleasure and the pride of being part Indian that he would have been deprived of: that would have been never really to know *what* he was.

It had come out despite them. Blood, they said, would out, and Indian blood, more powerful than any, would out though it were only a drop. There was an unseen power at work here. The spirits of his long-denied red forefathers had spoken to him at last (ironically enough, through his mother's own mouth) and claimed him as one of their own. Only who, exactly, were they? What was he? Indian, but what kind? Heir to what renown?

There was just one person who might be able to tell Jimmy the answers to his questions.

III

THAT HIS Grandfather Hawkins was half Indian, or more, was plain for all to see, yet Jimmy saw it for the first time when next the family went for a visit out to the farm. He who had been looking all his life for an Indian to adore!

But how were you to recognize the Indian in a man who dressed always in baggy, patched old denim overalls and a tattered denim jumper out at the elbows? Who, as Jimmy had seen, let his old wife cut his hair using an oatmeal bowl as a form instead of wearing it down to his shoulders in braids? Who when he came into town came not riding bareback on a horse but in a creaky old farmwagon drawn by a team of plodding gray mules? Sixty-five years of plowing, hoeing, picking cotton had taken all the noble savage out of the man.

"Grandfather," Jimmy said, "I've just been told that I am part Indian, and that I get it from you."

"Who told you?"

"My mother."

"Did, did she? Well, sonnyboy, our side of the family is ever bit as good as yore mother's, and you can tell her I said so. She's got a lot to brag about, now ain't she? Them Tylers. What did e'er a one of them ever amount to? Old Dub Tyler, jake-legged from all the bootleg corn liquor he's drank, in debt to everbody in town: he's something to be proud of, I reckon? That's yore other granddaddy. So any time yore mother's in the mood to trade compliments about—"

"What I want to know is, why didn't anybody ever tell me about this before?"

"I'd of told you if you'd ever of ast me. Whether yore mother liked it or not. Think I wouldn't? Tell anybody. Not that it's anybody else's business but my own. Son, what a man is born don't matter a hill of beans. It's what you make of yoreself that counts."

"If you're not what you are then what are you?" said Jimmy. "You're not anything. Tell me now about myself."

"Tell you what?"

"Tell about your father. My great-grandfather. The Indian."

"Why, what do you want to know about him?"

"Everything! I want to know all there is to know."

"Well, he was not what you would call a big man. Neither was he a little man. More what you would call middling-sized. Bothered with stomach trouble all his life, though what killed him was not that but something else. Died of—"

"What kind of Indian was he?"

"What do you mean, what kind of Indin was he?"

"I mean like Comanche, or Cheyenne, or Apache. You know. What tribe?

"Oh. Well, I wouldn't know nothing about that. Indin, that's all I can tell you, boy."

"What was his name?"

"His name? Mr. George P. Hawkins, same as mine."

"If he was an Indian, where did he ever get a name like that—Mr. George P. Hawkins? That's not an Indian name. Indians are named names like Rain-in-the-Face or Crazy Horse, or something like that. I expect he just never told you his true name."

"Must of been a Hawkins in the woodpile back somewheres along the line, just where and when I can't tell you, cause I wasn't there myself. I can tell you one thing though: I'm grateful I haven't had to go through life named George P. Crazy Horse. Yes, sir, I'm sure grateful I haven't had to go through—"

"How about your grandfather? Tell me about him."

"Never knowed the man. Dead 'fore ever I was born."

"Didn't your father ever tell you about him when you were a boy?"

"When I was a boy I never had no time to waste setting around talking about my granddaddy. And I ain't got none for it now. Maybe he was the Hawkins."

Another renegade. It ran in the family. Jimmy felt he had much to atone for.

IV

Before the coming of the white man, the northeastern part of Texas where Jimmy Hawkins lived with his father and mother was the domain of the Caddo Indians. The local tribe was one which, although he was born and raised there, and notwithstanding all his Indian lore, Jimmy had never heard of until he began delving into his pedigree.

To learn that he belonged to such an obscure tribe was a surprise, and for a moment something of a disappointment. He had rather set his heart on being a Comanche. However, he liked the name Caddo. He knew he was one: he felt a thrill of recognition the first time he read the word.

Specimens preserved in various museums, he read in the small guide book in the small town library, proved the Caddoes to have been the most talented potters of all the Indians of North America.

But who were their famous chiefs? Who were the Caddo Pontiac, the Caddo Sitting Bull, the Caddo Geronimo? Who were their most renowned warriors? Where were their great battles fought?

The Caddoes it was, he read, who had reared the numerous large burial mounds still to be found in that part of the state and adjacent Louisiana (in the one on his grandfather's farm did his own forefathers lie sleeping?), which, along with the name of nearby Caddo Lake, were at this late date (the book had been published in 1907) the only reminders left of this once large and powerful tribe.

Where had all the Caddoes gone?

Like the Mohicans, the Caddoes were no more. Their numbers depleted by their war against the white settlers, and by the diseases which the settlers brought with them, their last surviving remnant had been forcibly removed to Oklahoma in 1854 and resettled on government reservations, where, through intermarriage with and adoption into other tribes, the Caddoes had lost their separate identity.

The little book told no more; none other told as much. He had been orphaned of his entire nation. He was the last of the Caddoes.

V

WHAT Jimmy Hawkins had always known was now confirmed: he was meant for no common fate. He had been born with a horror of the ordinary, and had always known he was not what he seemed to the world to be. He had often wondered who he really was, and had felt that like the changeling prince in the fairy tale he had been cheated of his birthright and brought up in a meaner station of life than fate and his gifts had intended him for. The reason, as he now knew, was that he was the last of the Caddoes: rightful heir to all that he surveyed, with blood in his veins that cried out for vengeance: a dangerous person, a permanent threat to those who had wronged him. So they must have been warned by the bad fairy (herself Indian) who was not invited to his christening but who appeared at it all the same. "You may bleach him whiter than the snow, give him a white man's name, and bring him up in ignorance of his people," she had pronounced in a raspy voice, shaking a bony brown finger at them, "he is what he is. What will be will be." So Jimmy had always known he was ordained, marked out, chosen to perform some bold feat; now he knew it would be something to vindicate his dispossessed, destroyed, and all but forgotten race. He awaited the revelation of what it would be. Once he knew the name of his tribe he felt the constant presence of his red forebears molding him, training him, preserving him until such time as he should be ready and his mission be revealed to him.

They taught him to see what before he had overlooked, what others, outsiders, still overlooked: the relics everywhere of their immemorial stay in the land from which they had been driven out. In plowed fields they showed him arrowheads that generations of plowmen, though their eyes were seldom lifted from the ground, had not seen. In stones that the unknowing took to be just stones he recognized the mortars in which his people had ground their maize and the pestles with which they had pounded it, the flint knives with which they had skinned their game, the tomahawks with which they had brained their foes.

He felt them most powerfully in the woods. In the green stillness he could see their spirits flitting among the trees and in the whispering together of the branches could hear their voices. He knew no fear, for they were with him. They were the lords of the forest and he their only son, their sole survivor, the last arrow from the once-full quiver of their wrath. And when at home or at school he was whipped for his disobedience, they lent him fortitude. With them at his side he could endure without flinching whatever any white man could mete out. Not a whimper could they draw from him; he sneered in the faces of his tormentors. The last of the Caddoes brought no stain of dishonor upon the spirits of his proud dead.

If to be an Indian was a career in itself, to be the last of one's tribe was a calling. To be the sole repository of a nation's history, its traditions, its laws, its beliefs, and its rituals, and to know nothing of that history, those traditions, laws, beliefs, and rituals, and to be just twelve years old, was to carry an almost crushing weight of responsibility. No wonder Jimmy was aged and sober beyond his years. That with all this on his mind he should have no time for friends, for games, or for schoolbooks.

His confirmation time was fast approaching. He would turn thirteen that summer, would enter upon his man-

hood, and as soon as school was out Jimmy obeyed the call
he had heard to make a pilgrimage to his ancestral shrine:
the Caddo burial mound on his grandfather's farm. He
was to spend the summer in the country. His parents were
relieved to see him go, glad of a rest. The prospect of having him always about the house, of a whole long summer
of wrangling, was more than his mother could face. It was
his own idea; she need not accuse herself of getting rid of
him. After a few months' separation maybe they would
get along a little better. Hopefully, a summer in the open,
swimming, going fishing, exploring the farm, would make
a happier boy of him, a better pupil when school reopened
in the fall.

VI

"HE DON'T do a thing but dig in that damn dirt pile," his
grandfather reported when Jimmy's parents drove out to
celebrate his birthday. "He's at it all day long every day
and Sunday. Can't even get him to stop long enough to eat
his dinner. If you all weren't here he'd be out there right
now. Wouldn't you?" Over his shoulder the old man flung
a scowl at the great mound of earth that rose like a single
gigantic grave out of the field below the house.

"Well, I must say it seems to have done him good. He's
so changed I wouldn't have known him. Would you,
Mother?" said Jimmy's father, and turning to his wife, received a look that blazed with exasperation.

For no, she would not have known Jimmy, he was so
changed, and she was in torment while his father beamed.
It was not her boy but a stranger she found awaiting her,
a stranger whom she had brought into the world with her
pain on this day of the year. He had grown like a weed,
had in just these few weeks away from her shot up half a

head taller. The last of the baby fat had thinned from his cheeks, which now showed their bones, and his baby fairness was gone: he was as brown as a penny. No longer was he the soft round ungendered little sausage she remembered; his shoulders had wedged out, his little pot been trimmed away neat and flat and hard. The change in his chemistry had coarsened his skin, his hair, thickened his muscles, deepened his voice. Yet though his mother ached to be proud of his new manliness, she could not. She was no part of it. She was a little afraid of him. She felt the misgiving every mother feels when suddenly one day her son comes to present her with his bill for the many slights and indignities of his boyhood.

His manner confused and disarmed her. She had expected on his birthday to find him cocky and impertinent, and had come prepared to overlook it for the occasion. Her forbearance would not be wanted, thank you. Instead she found him subdued, withdrawn, grave. This gravity grated her as no amount of impudence would have done. How dared he treat her with such cool courtesy, as though there were no history of any troubles between them! To learn now that he had spent his time digging so fanatically in that old Indian mound instead of in the harmless pastimes she had imagined made her feel she had been betrayed and mocked.

"Must think he's going to find some buried treasure. Well, you're in for a big letdown if you do," said Jimmy's grandfather. "The Indins, why, they were all so piss-pore they never hardly had enough to eat, much less any silver or gold. What have you found? Just what I told you you'd find. Nothing but skeltons and a lot of old broken crocks."

Jimmy was used to his grandfather's disapproval of his project. The burial mound sat square in the middle of his grandfather's cotton patch. While Jimmy dug on top of the mound his grandfather chopped the cotton in the field below. Whenever the old man's progress down the row brought him parallel with the mound he would stop and rest and watch Jimmy dig. He refused ever to face the mound he would only lour at it over his shoulder, leaning on his hoe handle with one foot crossed over the other and his behind stuck out. But if the sight of his grandson's foolishness disgusted him, the sight of his grandfather's degradation filled Jimmy with shame and despair. Commanded by the voice of his people to know himself through knowing them, Jimmy had bared the buried history of the Caddoes, delving backwards in time from their end to their beginning. He had measured the antiquity of his lineage in countless shovelfuls of earth. The handiwork of his tribe had shown him the strangeness of his heritage, his own difference. From the mound's topmost layer, where the bodies, unceremoniously interred, had been so closely packed ("their numbers depleted by their war against the white settlers") that the bones were inseparably mixed, and where the little bones of children were numerous ("and by the diseases which the settlers brought with them"), he had dug down to the splendid rotting cerements, the broken, once-magnificent urns, the weapons of flint and obsidian worthy to accompany a great chief to the happy hunting grounds, of the days of their greatness: from desolation down to grandeur that made the desolation all the keener. Then to look down and see his grandfather, the man with more of the blood of the Caddoes in his veins than any other living man, hoeing his way down the rows of scraggly cotton: it was a constant reminder of how art the mighty fallen.

"I remember digging in there myself when I was a boy," said Jimmy's father. "I never found anything worth keeping."

"Maybe you didn't dig deep enough," said Jimmy.

"Why, what all have you found?"

"Oh, things."

"What sort of things?"

"Oh, just things."

"Well, some people collect old Indian things. Mr. Will Etheridge in town, for instance. He'll pay a dime apiece for flint arrowheads. Whole ones, that is, of course. I'll speak to him about you next time I see him. You can take and show him what you've found, see if he'll offer you something for it."

A laugh came from Jimmy's mother like the sound of breaking glass. "Jimmy isn't after buried treasure," she said. "And he wouldn't think of selling any of the things he's found. Would you, dear?" she said, turning to him with a spiteful simper. "They're sacred, isn't that right? Yes. You see, I'm the only one who understands, aren't I, my little Hiawatha? I can read you like an open book."

"Are we going to fight on my birthday, Mother?" asked Jimmy.

"Why, what better day for it?" she cried, regretting what she said even as she said it. "I was only trying to be friendly, but if you want to fight, what better day for it than your birthday?"

It was a shocking thing to say. She herself was quite taken aback. She had not known she was going to say that, it had just come out by itself. Thus she was all the more taken aback when Jimmy said, "I knew you were going to say that, Mother."

"He wants to work I'll put him to work and pay him for doing it," said Jimmy's grandfather. "Chopping cotton, fifty cents a day. It ain't near as hard work as spading in the ground. Fifty cents a day. Save it up and buy yoreself something nice. Damn foolishness to work for nothing when you could be earning pay. Buy yoreself a twenty-two rifle. A banjo. Get you a bicycle, then you can carry a paper route, earn money all year round. Tell you one thing, sonnyboy: prices of goods what they are today, if you was mine you wouldn't be out there wasting time when you could be bringing in a little something towards yore room and board and yore education."

Lest his wife say it first, Jimmy's father said he believed they could manage without that.

"Do you think I've grown, Mother?" asked Jimmy.

"I think you're looking thin," she said.

"I knew you were going to say that!" said Jimmy.

"Thin and flushed," she continued, ignoring the interruption. "Not well at all. I wonder if you're not coming down with something?" Truth was, she herself felt flushed and as though she might be coming down with something. She felt terribly out of sorts.

"It's because I'm excited," Jimmy said. "It's my birthday!"

He was excited. Something was going to happen. He had no inkling of what it would be—perhaps something not at all pleasant. But something momentous, he knew. It was imminent in the air like a break in the weather. This birthday would not end without bringing about some fundamental change in things.

"Well," said his mother, "you've had enough to be used to them and you've got a great many more to come. So you'd better begin calming down."

"But this one is special! This is my thirteenth birthday. Today I become a man."

"What! Is that what you think? Ha-ha! You've got a long way to go before you get to be a man, my son. You're still just a little boy. And I advise you not to forget it."

There was a birthday cake with fourteen candles—one to grow on—and when "Happy Birthday" had been sung Jimmy blew them all out with one breath. The presents were then opened and admired. Afterwards Jimmy's father said, first submitting a glance to his wife, "Yes, I can remember digging in that old mound myself when I was your age. Though like I say, I never had any luck. So you're interested"—another appeasing glance towards his wife—"in the Indians. Well, that's natural. Most boys are. Let's go and see just what you've been up to. Mother? Let's go and see what Jimmy's dug up, shall we?" He was being the peacemaker. Show a little interest in the boy's hobby, said the look to his wife, which Jimmy caught.

"You really don't want to see," said Jimmy.

"You mean you really don't want us to see," said his mother. "Well now, I think I do want to have a look. Maybe you've got hold of something you ought not to have."

"Why, Mother," said her husband. "What sort of thing could you have in mind?"

"I have in mind," she said, fixing him with her look, "something nasty. We all know what the Indians were like."

His indignation rose with a taste as sour as gorge. Yet she demeaned only herself. They were beyond her spite, as they were beyond her understanding; nothing she might say could smirch them. And he felt slightly dizzied. Again as previously he had known the instant before what his mother was about to say. He had actually heard her words seconds before they were spoken. It was like what happened sometimes with the phonograph, when you heard distantly the opening bars of the music before the record actually began to play. It had happened several times today, so that now Jimmy had the sense of being clairvoyant. It was as though he were in some sort of occult communication with his mother's unconscious mind. But if, for all her quarrelsomeness, his mother had been delivered into his power, Jimmy did not feel like gloating. It was too uncanny.

Once today his mother had read Jimmy's thoughts. He did not want his parents to visit the mound. Not for the reason his mother suspected but because it was hallowed ground and they were infidels who would profane it, the one with his idle curiosity, the other with her hatred and scorn. But both were determined now to be taken there, his father intent on making peace, his mother on making mischief.

She hated the thing, the mound, on sight. Before, hearing of Jimmy's dedication to it, she had viewed it as no more than a red rag of his meant to taunt her with. But seeing it sitting there so squat and alien and old she hated it. Brown and bare, it rose like a single enormous grave out of the field of dazzling white cotton. That it was man-made was obvious; no one could ever have mistaken it for a natural mound. Rectangular in form, it stretched two hundred feet, was fifty feet wide, rose twenty feet from the ground. She pictured the dead savages inside it packed like sardines in a tin, and she shuddered with revulsion. Such promiscuous burial offended her as not only uncivilized but obscene. If she had her way these ugly reminders of barbarism would all be leveled to the ground. And her son was under its spell. She could see it working in the dark depths of his eyes. It was an atavism in him, a taint in his blood.

But the place had a power. Undeniably it did, if even she was forced to acknowledge it. Standing to adjust her vision inside the black shadow it cast upon the glaring cotton she could feel its solemn spell. The single grave of a whole clan of people! She felt herself belittled by its bulk and its antiquity, and despite herself, reverent. She could gauge the power it had to attract her son by the power it had to repel her. Her sight sharpened and she saw him going ahead, his pace quickening with each step, drawn to it like an iron filing to a magnet, and her heart misgave her. She felt they were hopelessly sundered. As if a snake had coiled at her feet to strike, she sensed something stir somewhere nearby. The sensation was overpowering that her approach had alerted the hostile hosts of the dead. Her courage, born of her contempt, forsook her, and for a moment she stood quaking with superstitious dread.

Jimmy's father was impressed by the size of the opening he had made in the mound. More than impressed, he was awed, dumbfounded. Starting at about the middle of one of the long sides, at the spot where, on his first visit to the mound, he had received the command to dig, he had removed a slice six feet wide and six feet deep all the way down to the base. There was nothing slipshod, nothing boyish about his excavation; it was all quite amazingly professional-looking, like a photograph in *The National Geographic*, which was where he must have gotten his ideas from, of a field camp on the site of a "dig" of an archaeological expedition. He must have dug furiously, almost frantically, and yet his cuttings had been made systematically and with care—indeed, they had been made with reverence; his findings sorted and labeled and catalogued. To house them he had erected a tent on top of the mound. He had cut in the face of it a flight of steps leading there.

On the tent floor laid out in rows were neat stacks of human bones each crowned by its grinning gap-toothed skull. With each stack was carefully preserved its owner's beaded medicine bag, his tomahawk, his clay pipe, and in those cases where it had survived intact, the pouch containing parched corn that was to have fed him on his journey to the happy hunting grounds. Being but freshly unearthed, the skulls were not bleached white but were still a waxen yellow. To some adhered coverings of pursed brown skin drawn back from toothless gums in everlasting howls. Nobody to hear them but one thirteen-year-old boy of mixed blood and divided loyalties. And his was but one of many such mounds. They were numerous throughout that part of the state and adjacent Louisiana. Sights for tourists, spots for picnickers, curio seekers. On their slopes children romped and around their bases farmers gathered their crops while a nation groaned underground and no one heard. Only he heard. To him each and every skull he uncovered screamed its plea for pity, its demand for justice. It all came down to him. He was all they had. His heart was their last war drum; on it they beat night and day.

Asked by his father what he meant to do with all these Jimmy replied that he meant to put them back where he found them.

Put them back? his father wondered.

Wasn't that what he would do? One of those might be his great-great-grandfather.

In her hands Jimmy's mother held a clay jug, one of the few he had managed to salvage unbroken. Perfect in condition, perfect in form and in decoration, it demanded to be picked up and handled, demanded it even of a person in whom it produced an aversion exceeding what she felt in looking at the grimacing yellow skulls. It seemed fresh from the hand that had made it centuries ago. The design was of diamonds in bands that coiled about it shrinking and expanding in conformity with its shape, a treatment that must have been suggested to the potter by his own procedure in coiling his rope of clay. If, as has been said, the soul of a people is to be found in its pottery, then the soul of the mound builders, as expressed in this piece, was one of boundless self-assurance, superb and haughty, implacable and utterly without remorse, possessed of some inner harmony that gave them a careless mastery of life. Unconquerable, the spirit of the people who could produce one such thing!

She tore her eyes from it to look at her son. He stood gazing at the vessel in her hand with an expression that shrank her heart. There was nothing of pleasure, nothing of fond possession in his look—rather the reverse: a look of his belonging body and soul to it, and an ineffable sadness: the look a priest might give to the chalice of the mass or the reliquary of the founder of his order. A shudder of revulsion shook her soul, she dashed the jug to the ground, where it burst like a grenade, and as Jimmy drew back— for he had already heard the words she was about to utter —she hissed, "A snake in your mother's bosom, that's what you are! A snake in your mother's bosom!"

They stood staring into one another's eyes in mute wonder. She was merely aghast, but he was both aghast and enlightened. What was to have happened had happened. On his thirteenth birthday an Indian boy becomes a brave, a man, and is given his man's name. The spirits of his ancestors, speaking through their enemy's own mouth, had just told him his.

VII

Snake-in-His-Mother's-Bosom, in whose new name was contained his mission, returned home in September after his summer in the country most unwillingly. He dreaded ever to see his mother again. He was not afraid of his mother, he was afraid for her, and thus for himself.

He knew now that his mother's telling him about his Indian blood had been no accident. She had been tricked into it against her will by her enemies, the spirits of his dead tribesmen. And he knew why. If he had not known before, he knew now, after excavating the mound—that hive that like hornets had lived and died all for one and one for all. Digging down through layer upon layer, generation upon generation, he had come to know the importance to them of preserving the tribal continuity, the sacrilege it would be to them should ever the chain be broken, especially in its last link. He knew now how inexhaustible was the Indian patience in waiting for revenge, the refinements of Indian cruelty in exacting it. He had not read these things written on buckskin or bark or carved in stone. He had seen them in the grin of Indian skulls, in the incisions on Indian jugs, in those geometric designs endlessly repeated that always came full circle, returning in the end to their source. His mother's crime against them was to have brought him up in ignorance of them. For this she must be made to pay, and Indian justice decreed that her punishment was that her son be a snake in her bosom, Indian subtlety that out of her own mouth must come the discovery that he was theirs, that she herself must bestow upon him his tribal name, that out of her very mouth must come— That was what he dreaded. What message would they next transmit through her to him? Not knowing what she was saying, what would she say next?

One thing his mother was determined never to say again was that he was a snake in her bosom. She regretted saying that. It was a terrible thing to say. Dreadful! She had meant to hurt him, and could see that she had; but not nearly as much as she had hurt herself. What made it doubly awful was that it was also rather laughable. Stiff, stagey, like something out of an old-fashioned play, like "Never darken my doorway again!"—not at all her usual way of expressing herself. And this comical old-fashioned stiffness somehow made the memory of it all the more embarrassingly painful. Her excuse was, she had not really meant to say it. She had gotten carried away and it had just popped out. If only she could have kept her vow never to repeat it! Before he had been back home two days, however, she did, provoked by his sullen refusal to answer to his name.

But that was not his name. Not any more. He was Jimmy Hawkins no longer and never again would he answer to that name. When called by it, at home or at school,

he would await silently and with a maddening little smile
the question or the command that followed, but he would
not answer to that name though beaten for his surliness
until the principal's arm ached, until his father begged him
to be allowed to quit. Hostile as he felt towards his mother,
she was still his mother, and even the last of the Caddoes
shrank from his terrible new appellation. But his people
had spoken. Snake-in-His-Mother's-Bosom they had called
him: Snake-in-His-Mother's-Bosom he must be. That the
name fit him he had to admit. It fit him like a skin. And
painful though it was, there was also strong medicine in
the name. It encased him in an armor of scales. It enabled
him to slink in silence. It gave to his brain the serpent's
subtlety. It equipped him with a forked tongue for speaking to the enemies by whom he was surrounded. It armed
him with fangs.

Because he would respond to none other, his mother was
often goaded into calling him a name that was painful to
her. Thus things went from bad to worse.

They could not be together for half a day now without
a quarrel breaking out. Though she charged him with being
the one who always started it, in fact it was she herself.
In dread of what she might say, he wanted peace, no more
quarrels. Yet he was Snake-in-His-Mother's-Bosom. And of
course when riled he struck back. But she began it. The
spirits egged her on.

It was as if, that day in the country, his birthday, they
had lured her, using her very hatred of them as bait, to
their mound, where, like a host of germs entering the blood-
stream through some scratch, they had stolen inside her.
Now she was like a person unconscious that a fatal disease
is quietly eating him alive, as cancer is said to be painless
and give no warning until its host is already past cure. In
this case the organ invaded was the soul.

To watch them play with their victim was both horrible

and fascinating. That he was himself a part of their scheme he knew, but was powerless to prevent. Besides, he rather enjoyed it. By making him remind her continually of them they rubbed her where she was rawest. Drop by drop the cup of her irritation would fill, then at some trifle brim over. Then she tore at her hair as though there were bats in it. Then she would not have peace. Then nothing so irritated her as his efforts to appease her. "You're good at starting trouble, aren't you?" she would taunt him. "But when the going gets rough you cry off. Soft! Can't take it, eh?" She would not let him give in to her. He shunned her; this enraged her. He fleeing, she pursuing, their arguments swept up and down stairs and through all the rooms of the house, doors banging, windows, walls, and furniture shuddering at the violence. He could not shake her off; she clattered after, attaching herself to him like a tin can tied to a dog's tail. When she had him cornered then he turned. Then he bared his fangs. They parried words. She always won, always had the last word: it put them in her mouth. And when she had said something at last that chilled him into silence, then she would quit the field in dubious triumph. For days, weeks—the torture was fiendishly drawn out—all their quarrels would end on the same double-edged phrase. So it had been from the start, with "That's the Indian in you coming out!" So it was later with "A snake in your mother's bosom, that's what you are!" So it was for a time with "I brought you into the world just to torment me!" Then, wrought to a pitch of outrage which that phrase had grown too worn to express, she would utter a new and more reckless one, something that left them both appalled, then retire to savor the bitter taste of her triumph. So she was led on from one Pyrrhic victory to another.

As he grew more morose she grew more cutting. "Aren't you the little joy to your mother, though? Mother's little joy! Other women's children bring sunshine and laughter into the house, but you, sullen creature—! You're a stranger in the house. You came into the world just to torment me, you snake in your mother's bosom, you little savage, you!" And he would glower at her out of those hooded cold black eyes, remote, hostile, alien, lashing her on to ever more bitter recriminations, drawing the net ever closer about herself, until in a fit of rage one day she said, "You will be the death of me!"

So ended the worst quarrel they had ever had, with both of them left gasping for breath. This time she feared she had gone really too far. Ah, but she had certainly given him something to think about! That she could see. As in the days when she used to wash him, her words had wiped his face clean of its black scowl, leaving him pale and blinking. In tones still more ominous she repeated, "You will be the death of me!"

VIII

UNDER COVER of darkness Snake-in-His-Mother's-Bosom fled from home that night, never to return. He went to seek for himself a new home, new parents, a new name. He knew where to find them. Where not to be found by the ones he was leaving behind.

To postpone the discovery of his flight he left a dummy of himself in his bed as jailbreakers do. It looked so much like him lying there in his bed it made him feel it really was himself, the old him with all his troubles, with that heavy curse upon him, that he was leaving behind. By the time his trick was found out and chase given, he would be beyond recapture.

His mother would fume and rage when she found him gone. Doubting prophetess, eager victim, she would pursue her appointed executioner and be angry when he eluded her. Then having done her duty she would give up the search. His mother would receive condolences from family and friends, and look sad, and be secretly glad, and never know how much she had to be glad for.

The route taken by Snake-in-His-Mother's-Bosom was the same one along which the last surviving remnant of his people had been driven in 1854. His destination was the same as theirs. Across the Red River in Oklahoma among those Indian tribes with whom the earlier Caddoes exiled from Texas had found a home, and lost their identity, the last of the Caddoes hoped to find for himself a new home, a new mother and father, or many mothers, many fathers, lose his identity, and thereby evade his terrible fate. A Comanche, a Cherokee, a Choctaw, or a Creek: when Snake-in-His-Mother's-Bosom had been adopted as one or another of those and been given his new name then the Caddoes would truly be no more.

No more! The night around him groaned at the dismal thought. The moon veiled her face behind a cloud and through the treetops passed a long low sigh of woe. Over the dark land of the Caddoes the sentence of irrevocable doom rolled out in the muffled drum of the owl.

The road to the river and the ferry to Oklahoma, the road he was on, would take him within two miles of his grandfather's farm. Could Snake-in-His-Mother's-Bosom pass so near and not pay a last visit to his ancestral burial mound? At this season, early spring, before time for the planting of crops, his grandparents slept late. He could go and pay his respects and still get away unseen. Although it was from their prophecy that he was fleeing, the last of the Caddoes must not go forever from the land of his fathers without taking leave of his tutelary spirits.

He arrived shortly before daybreak. The house was still asleep as he passed it going down to the mound. In the field still stood the stalks of last year's cotton. A multitude of empty cottonbolls murmured in the wind. Day broke as he stepped on top of the mound. He advanced to the center and set down his suitcase. Looking at the ground he seemed to see into it, down into the depths where he had dug, down to the bottommost layer where the old first fathers lay in their lavish decay, smiling serenely, confident of the continuity of their kind, having gone into the grave before the white man's coming. Above them in successive layers of decline, those who had followed after: children laid on top of their parents, their children on top of them, and now on top of all himself, the last of the line, come to forswear his allegiance and bid them goodbye forever.

He prepared to deliver his farewell speech, and the silence grew attentive. He was about to begin when a sound, a rustle, at his back made him turn. From a hole in the ground quite near him a snake was emerging slowly like something being squeezed out of a tube. Out and out it came: its final four inches were rattles. It was an old snake. Its skin was dull and lusterless, its markings blurred, and it was half blind with a film clouding its eyes so that it groped its way with its tongue flickering constantly, tasting the air for unseen danger. It hitched itself along in angles as the knight moves on a chessboard. It passed within mere feet of him while he stood rigid and unbreathing. Yet he was not afraid of being bitten by the snake. No snake would bite him. He was of the clan of snakes. He was a snake himself. It was something else that he feared. This was the time of year when the ground's warming up roused snakes from their winter's sleep and brought them out. But in the emergence of this old, decrepit, possibly dying one coinciding with his visit here he feared some omen.

Every few feet the snake paused and half coiled itself to strike and reared its head and peered blindly about, its long forked tongue quivering like an antenna. Presently it came up against a stone. At once it began stroking its jaw against this stone. He could hear the rasping of its scales.

And suddenly with one long stroke, at the part dividing its nostrils, the snake's skin split and out of its dull wrapper popped a bright new head with keen new eyes that blinked at the raw daylight. Then rapidly it peeled itself its entire length, turning the old skin inside out as a finger comes out of a glove. Its glassy little scales tightly woven in a pattern of diamonds, it resembled nothing so much as a belt of Indian beadwork. A shiver of pleasure ran down from its head to its rattles as it felt the air for the first time on its new skin. It gaped, showing its fangs, coiled and reared itself high and slowly looked about with lordly menace. Then quick as a fish it flashed away and was gone.

Snake-in-His-Mother's-Bosom knelt and picked up the cast-off skin. Rising, he saw his mother's face appear over the top of the mound. He felt himself instinctively coil, his lips fly back to bare his fangs. "Ah-hah," said his mother's smirk, "I knew where to find you, didn't I? You can't get away from me."

Beneath his feet all was silence. Silence and sly toothless grins.

Snake-in-His-Mother's-Bosom surrendered himself with a sigh to his fate. He could not get away from her—foolish ever to have thought he could. He was what he was; what would be would be. The snake might shed his skin, but only to grow another one the same as before.

In obedience to his victim's nod, Snake-in-His-Mother's-Bosom took up his suitcase and followed her down the steps and across the barren field to the car. In its rearview mirror he watched the mound diminish and finally disappear. The snakeskin rode on his lap. Now he must wait. Must wait for their next, their final command. It would not come soon; they sipped their pleasures slowly. Many times yet he would have to hear his mother say that he would be the death of her. So many times that when the final order came it would be almost welcome, a release. Distant and ghostly, it sounded already in the echoing silence of his mind. Over and over, like a phonograph record when the needle cannot find the starting groove. "Kill me at once then and be done with it!" his mother's voice was saying. One day the needle would find the groove. Then out would come the command loud and clear and with the sudden shock of long-expectedness. Then Snake-in-His-Mother's-Bosom would strike, accomplish his mission and fulfill the phophecy; and then at last the ghosts of the Caddoes could lie down at peace in their many-tiered mound and haunt the land and him no more.

A Note on the Type

THE TEXT of this book was set in a typeface called Primer, designed by Rudolph Ruzicka for the Mergenthaler Linotype Company and first made available in 1949. Primer, a modified modern face based on Century broadface, has the virtue of great legibility and was designed especially for today's methods of composition and printing.

Primer is Ruzicka's third typeface. In 1940 he designed Fairfield, and in 1947 Fairfield Medium, both for the Mergenthaler Linotype Company.

Ruzicka was born in Bohemia in 1883 and came to the United States at the age of eleven. He attended public schools in Chicago and later the Chicago Art Institute. During his long career he has been a wood engraver, etcher, cartographer, and book designer. For many years he was associated with Daniel Berkeley Updike and produced the annual keepsakes for The Merrymount Press from 1911 until 1941.

Ruzicka has been honored by many distinguished organizations, and in 1936 he was awarded the gold medal of the American Institute of Graphic Arts. From his home in New Hampshire, Ruzicka continues to be active in the graphic arts.

This book was designed by Victoria Dudley
and composed, printed, and bound
by The Haddon Craftsmen, Inc.,
Scranton, Pennsylvania